SIN, SUGAR AND SHADOWS

LILA HARROW: A POINT MUSE COZY PARANORMAL MYSTERY BOOK THREE

KELLY ETHAN

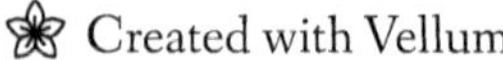 Created with Vellum

Sin, shadows, and a dessert duel. Let the mayhem begin.

Lila Harrow, baker witch extraordinaire, knew when the banshee hollered, death soon followed.

She just didn't expect the death to be her beloved bakery, Hearts Delight. But when two sinful, dark witches open a dessert bakery across the road, the cakes start dropping and so do the corpses.

Lila has no choice but to sleuth up and join the food fight fray.

A piece of cake for a witchy baker.

If you like snarky dialogue, murder, and mayhem then you'll love the third installment in Kelly Ethan's Point Muse Cozy Paranormal Mystery spin off series – Lila Harrow: A Point Muse Cozy Paranormal Mystery.

<u>Unlock the mayhem of Sin, Sugar and Shadows.</u>

ONE

"Can we storm the building yet? Have the kidnappers contacted us with their demands?"

Lila Harrow, baker, witch, and owner of *Heart's Delight Bakery* eyed her overly militaristic grand-mother. "They haven't kidnapped anyone yet... That we know of." Lila refused to stare out her front window at the looming threat of the grand opening of the *Devilish Dessert Bakery*.

"They kidnapped your future business and are holding it hostage with their fluttering eyelashes and flirty smiles." Elspeth hoisted her sagging camouflage pants and pointed out her green-painted face. "See this? This is how we need to proceed. Military action. Swift and decisive. Run those witches out of town."

"Yeah, you dames kinda need to do something. Those eyelashes got you beat." Colin, the mouthy pug and incidentally, the wicked witch's minion, waddled into the bakery. Green patches spotted his cream fur.

"Elspeth? Why is Colin covered in green mange?" asked banshee, witch-hybrid Holly Harrow, who also happened to be one of Lila's cousins. She took a few steps away from the advancing plague pug. "Is it catchy? I have a heavy day at work and can't afford to be sick."

Lila snorted. "You work at a funeral home. A heavy workday for you is bad for everyone else." For a death obsessed banshee, working in a funeral home was a dream job. But lately, Holly seemed worn out and more whiny than normal for a Harrow.

"You have no idea." Holly ran a hand through her normally sleek, brown, chin-length hair and disturbed her bangs. "And I don't see why you're all stressing about the Devlin's. More choice in Point Muse is a good thing."

Lila gasped and held a hand over her heart. "Are you trying to induce a heart attack? Those dessert wenches will drive my business away. Just ask Elspeth." Lila poked a finger at her grandmother. "She has past experience with that family."

Elspeth nodded somberly, then ruined the effect with a cackle that caused the lights overhead to flicker. "The family's bad news, especially their grandmother, Delilah Devlin. A black-hearted crony who'd steal your marriage, heart, and business in a heartbeat." Elspeth scowled. "You stay away from those girls, Colin. You're mine and I'm never letting you go. Got it, pug?"

"Sweet cheeks, you say the sweetest things." Colin brushed against Elspeth's camo-colored pant leg.

Holly shuddered. "That sounded more like a threat than sweet mutterings to me. Besides, the dessert bakery hasn't opened yet. How bad could it be?"

"It's all about intent and the Devlin family intend to crush their competition in the most dark and heinous way possible... With sinful flirting." Elspeth stomped to the window and whipped out her binoculars, peering at the bakery.

"Do I want to know where you hid those binoculars?" Lila eyed her grandmother. Elspeth had dressed for war. From the green on her face to her camouflage-colored jogging suit, to the tips of her color-coordinated combat boots and matching long green wig, her grandmother was ready to rumble.

Elspeth tore her attention away from the bakery and focused on Lila. "You need to get your head in the game, soldier. There's nothing more evil than a dark witch with mayhem in her heart and sin in her soul."

"Did you just describe yourself?" Holly pasted an innocent expression on her face.

"Death wish." Lila coughed into her hand.

The door to the bakery slammed open and another of Lila's cousins, Xandie Meyers, stood framed in the doorway. A slight breeze ruffled Xandie's shoulder-length, fuzzy brown hair, and her amber eyes gleamed. All the Harrow women shared the same-colored eyes and brown hair. Lila, the eldest, tallest, and curviest, was the family drama queen or drama llama as they'd named her. Xandie, next in the pecking order, stood at an average height, had an obsession with sugar, and been appointed the Librarian to the supernatural Great Library of Alexandria. Stubborn, quick to act, and a total bookworm, Xandie had only discovered her Harrow family and her missing mother a year ago. Holly, the youngest, shortest, and skinniest of the family, was a banshee, witch-hybrid and obsessed with death. *And* the quietest of the lot... Until she mouthed off to their grandmother, Elspeth, the wicked witch of

Point Muse, who had an unhealthy love of glaringly bright wigs.

"We have a problem." Xandie shut the door behind her and held her chest as she took a shuddering breath.

"When don't we?" Lila rolled her eyes and gestured to a chair. "Take a seat and tell us about our next calamity."

Xandie sagged into a chair. "This one involves two blind men and a hammer."

"Sounds right up my alley." Elspeth dropped her binoculars onto the windowsill and faced her granddaughters.

"Just tell us, so I can run away and hide." Holly glared at her cousin.

Xandie paused dramatically before rushing her words out. "Braun and Grim are over at the dessert bakery helping the twins renovate the apartment upstairs." Xandie waited for the room's reaction.

"So? Hopefully, they're paid in desserts." Holly licked her lips. "I heard their blueberry pie's amazing."

Elspeth slapped a hand on the windowsill. "See. It's started already. Divide and flirt. This is their modus operandi. We need a war council ASAP."

"Everyone, calm down." Lila pinched the bridge

of her nose. Matthew Grim, reaper, had stumbled into Point Muse a little while ago. But he'd quickly wormed his way into her life and bakery. He even shared her office space and lived upstairs above her bakery. "Grim is an adult. He can do whatever he wants." Even if it was hanging out with her bakery competition.

Elspeth snorted. "Since when is a Harrow woman calm in the face of a philandering boyfriend?"

"Big word, Elspeth. But he isn't philandering. He's renovating." *She hoped.* They'd only started spending time together recently and, so far, he hadn't run screaming in the opposite direction of her family. Surely a duo of flirty, dark witch bakers wouldn't turn his head.

"You say potato." Elspeth shrugged and returned to her bakery stalking.

"Well, I for one am not happy." Xandie poked her bottom lip out and pouted. "And I told him exactly that, but he thinks I'm letting Elspeth corrupt me with her paranoia."

Hey," Elspeth protested. "It ain't paranoia if they're really after you, and the Devlins have form. I rest my case."

Colin waddled up to Elspeth and she hoisted

him onto her hip so he could peer outside. "Baker girl has another problem."

Lila thumped her head onto the table. "What now?"

"I wondered why it was so quiet around here." Colin waved a paw at the other bakery. "We have a traitor in the fam."

All three girls rushed to the window, gasping as a large black dog looked up and down the street, before trotting over to the dessert bakery and pawing at the door.

Lila gasped again as the door opened and Nash pranced inside. "That little hellhound... *That's it.* There's only so much a Harrow can handle." Lila dusted off her hands and stormed out the door.

"*Woo hoo.* Fight. Fight. Fight." Elspeth bounced on her feet like a prizefighter as she chanted.

Holly dragged Elspeth back and slammed the door shut, giving Lila a thumbs up.

"Steal my dog, will you. Face Harrow wrath." Lila raised a fist and thumped on the *Devilish Dessert's* door. She gritted her teeth and braced for a fight.

The door swung open. A short woman in her mid-20s, with sparkly violet eyes and long black curly hair, looked up at her. "I'm sorry, but we aren't open yet. The grand opening's only a few days away, though." She shot a dazzling smile up at Lila and started to close the door.

Lila quickly shoved her somewhat large, sneaker-shod foot in the door, bracing it open. "I'm not here about your bakery. You have my hellhound inside."

"Oh, he is such a cutie." The woman flung the door open and waved Lila inside. "And it's such a smart idea to have his name engraved on that little medallion attached to his collar. Nash sure does love our blueberry pie. Come in, just ignore the mess. We're still getting set up."

"I bet he does," Lila muttered under her breath. Her traitor dog was in for a world of trouble when she got hold of him.

The other woman offered her hand. "Forgot to introduce myself. I'm Ruby Devlin and you must be Lila Harrow from *Heart's Delight* bakery across the road."

Lila gingerly took the woman's hand and twitched it in a fake greeting. Her hand swallowed the other woman's completely. Made her feel like a giant. "I know who you are."

Ruby dropped her hand and trilled a husky laugh. "Of course, you do. Being a Harrow, I'm sure you've heard about my family. But we just want to make desserts. You'll have no trouble with us." She winked and led Lila through the bakery to the kitchen.

Lila pretended not to notice, but the glaring differences between the two bakeries were obvious. Heart's Delight had a stone hearth that dominated the room, white tables and chairs spread around the room, and a comfy sofa or two near the fire. Cozy and heartwarming, the bakery cheered her up as soon as she took a step inside. Devilish Desserts on the other hand was all about glamour. Marble-top tables, wooden stools, and white subway tiles made the area look glossy, modern. There was even a glowing chandelier suspended in pride of place from the ceiling.

"Too much for Point Muse?" Ruby opened the door to a kitchen that looked remarkably like Lila's.

Not to mention her own hellhound chowing down on a slice of blueberry pie from a pretty pink china plate.

Nash's entire body twitched as he slowly turned his head toward Lila. "Pie good," he grumbled at her and dropped his head to lick up the last of the blueberry pie.

Her coal-black hellhound had been a gift from her father, Shade, and his boss, Hades, God of the

Underworld. A duo of escaping demon hag sisters had headed for Point Muse and since Nash was the runt of the three-headed dog Cerberus's litter, the dodgy God of the Underworld had gifted him to Lila for protection. Until now, it'd been a match made in Elysian Fields. Lila crossed her arms. "Since when did you take food from strangers? What have I told you about that?"

"Pie good, "Nash repeated and went back to cleaning his plate.

"Sorry. We just thought he was so cute." Another woman, the exact image of Ruby Devlin, walked out of the pantry.

"This is my twin sister, Rose." Ruby performed the introduction. "We didn't think it'd be an issue feeding him. He's so adorable." Ruby ruffled Nash's ears, then gathered the plate up and placed it on the bench.

"It's Point Muse. There's always an issue or a poison or two floating around. He knows better."

Nash whined and slunk over to Lila.

"Point Muse *is* quite a busy town." Rose leaned against the counter.

"And now we have two bakeries," Lila muttered.

"I'm sure there's enough business for both of us." Ruby beamed at Lila. "I heard there's a birthday party at the retirement village. Obviously, there's plenty of sweet lovers in Point Muse."

Lila smiled slowly, fighting a victory smirk. "That's true. I'm catering the party."

Ruby nodded. "Good for you. But I'm sure there's plenty of work to be had here in Point Muse for both businesses."

"As long as the town doesn't serve up another murder, we should all be fine."

"Point Muse does have a certain reputation," Rose agreed with Lila.

"Welcome to the murder capital of the supernatural world."

The women looked at each other and smirked. "We were actually referring to the Harrow name, not the body count."

Always comes back to Elspeth. Lila prowled around the kitchen, past the open pantry door. She glanced in with professional curiosity. Rows of small, stoppered bottles with different colored herbs lined shelf after shelf. What dessert bakery needed so many herbs?

Rose stepped in front of Lila and shut the pantry door. "Can't give away all our secrets now." She winked at Lila then exchanged a longer glance with her twin.

Aha. Secrets being the key word. Lila smiled sweetly. "Of course not. Secrets are the main business of Point Muse, anyway. Just be careful, they have a way of coming out with a bang."

"Don't tell me you're threatening these sweet women, Lila Harrow?"

Zach Braun, Point Muse's police chief, bear shifter, and Xandie's boyfriend, stood in the doorway glowering at Lila.

A sheepish-looking Matthew Grim hovered behind him.

Lila raised an eyebrow at the men. "Why, Chief Braun and Matthew Grim, what a surprise to see you here. I was just explaining the quirks of Point Muse to our newest residents. No threat here."

"I hope not. We're an inclusive town and all are welcome."

Lila nodded in agreement with Braun's words. "Absolutely, and in the nature of inclusivity, I'd like to point out that your somewhat crabby girlfriend is waiting at my bakery. Something about a missed date?"

"Date? We had a date?" Braun looked flustered and handed Grim his hammer. "Sorry, ladies. I need to... I mean..."

"You need to go now. Especially since Xandie's currently hanging out with Elspeth."

"Right." Braun spun around and bolted out of the kitchen.

"Goodness, look how fast a motivated man can run." Lila turned back to the twins. "Thanks for looking after Nash, but I can take it from here." With a nod, she grabbed Nash by the collar and hauled him out of the bakery. She breathed a sigh of relief when the door closed behind her.

"Did Braun really have a date with Xandie?" Matthew stood next to Lila on the sidewalk, his gray eyes twinkling down at her.

Hecate, curse the way-too-appealing man. She wanted to be mad at him, but something about the tall, wide shouldered man with a big beaky nose distracted her. "She's definitely crabby."

"She's got Harrow blood, that's a given." Matthew walked beside Lila as they crossed the road in front of her bakery.

"Are we still on for dinner at Mayweather Inn?"

"Tonight?"

"How about in a couple of days? I still have a lot of paperwork to finish and..."

"And you have a renovation to help with and you want to swing your hammer," Lila replied snidely.

"That's Braun's hammer, I'm just the support crew." He eyed Lila. "Jealous?"

Lila coughed and spluttered. "Nope. But if I were you, I'd be careful hanging out with those women."

"Why would that be?"

"Because, according to Elspeth, there's nothing worse than a dark witch with mayhem in her heart and sin on her soul. And this is Point Muse. We all know how mayhem ends..."

With a murder.

TWO

"Dragons do not come cheap, Lila Harrow." Es Penne, teenage dragon and sometimes bakery assistant, flicked a long strand of black hair over her shoulder. "Besides, now there's another bakery in town, maybe I'll get a pay rise." Es waggled her eyebrows at Lila.

"Don't get your hopes up." Lila reached into the back of her brightly colored bakery van and drew out three cardboard boxes full of iced cupcakes. "Take these *Vanilla Viagra for the Soul* cupcakes to the retirement home. They have a lounge set up for Marcy's birthday party."

Groaning, Es juggled the cake boxes. "Just think about the pay rise."

"Your grandmother's the matriarch of the

Pendrakon clan and sits on a literal golden hoard. Ask her for a pay rise."

Es snorted. "She believes that old-fashioned stuff about working for your money. I'd much rather deal with you."

"Then mush, minion. Earn your keep." Lila waved the mercenary pay-raise-seeker away with a flap of her hand.

The teenage dragon groaned and trudged inside the Eternal Springs Retirement Home.

A bright red sports car zoomed into the car park and squealed into a place next to Lila's van.

"Talk about a car screaming *"look at me."* Lila curled her lip. Give her a solid, dependable van any day. Grabbing the last of the cake boxes, Lila slammed the van door closed and spun around, narrowly missing the tall, skinny, bottle-blonde prancing past on spindly killer heels.

"Watch it, cake girl. This dress cost more than what you've got on *and* your van put together." The brassy blonde sidestepped Lila, gave her the evil eye, then pranced inside the retirement home.

"Oh yeah, this day's gonna be great. I can feel it." Taking a deep breath to calm her nerves, Lila marched toward the entrance of the home. The sound of a revving engine drew her attention. As did the glossy black van, a similar size to her own. Except this one had *Devilish Desserts* emblazoned on the side. "Scoping the competition out. Why am I not surprised?" The two smiley Devlin twins talked a good game about lots of work for both bakeries, but here they were, stalking Lila.

"Is there a reason you're lurking in the car park, Ms. Harrow?" inquired a woman in her early fifties, sporting shiny auburn hair and super-long matching red nails.

"Nope, just avoiding speeding cars and stalking competitors."

"My mother only has a certain amount of energy. So, I'd appreciate it if you'd hurry up. We're on a timetable here."

Talk about impatient. Lila mustered a professional smile, nodded, and entered the home, heading for the lounge. "The client is always right. The client is always right." She repeated her mantra over and over.

"I see you've met my daughter, Laura-Jean." A fragile, elderly woman with gray hair offered Lila a small smile. "She means well, but when that horrible Chastity comes around, she loses all sense."

"Would Chastity be a skinny blonde with lethal

heels and a love of fast red cars?" Lila placed the boxes on the table and motioned for Es to unpack.

"Yes. Horrible woman. She's an acquaintance of my daughter. Chastity's ex-husband is the Pastor here in Point Muse." The elderly woman held a gnarled hand out. "I'm Marcy Upshot."

"Ah, the birthday girl." Lila gently took the woman's hand in a loose grip before releasing it "Thank you for choosing *Heart's Delight bakery* to cater your party."

"I'm addicted to your cupcakes. The big cake is mainly to keep Laura-Jean happy. She thinks everyone should have an over-the-top birthday cake."

A three-tier chocolate mud cake with lavender icing and delicate blush pink roses covering every available inch definitely qualified as overdoing. But a job is a job. "Well, I hope you enjoy your cupcakes." Lila winked.

"As long as that snooty woman Chastity stays away from me I will." Marcy nodded and shuffled off toward the table groaning with sweets.

The aforementioned Chastity had the pastor in a quiet corner. She leaned into him and whispered intently.

Pastor Ezekiel Moss had set up shop in Point Muse a few months ago. The Church of the Repentant Creatures had a fanatical following among Point Muse's elderly supernatural set. Of which a large majority were women. The pastor's tall height, flippy dark hair with silver sides, and his warm smile, certainly helped. *And* the fact that he was now officially divorced from the sports-car-driving Chastity.

"It was my mother's choice to hire you. I favored the new dessert bakery. Fresh blood is always a bonus."

Laura-Jean scowled at Lila, pointing with a sharp-tipped red talon. "I'm also not impressed with the canine aspect of your business."

Lila followed the pointing finger to the corner of the room where Nash held court with the elderly residents. "Nash has been approved by the health department and is on the books at the home as a service dog. He has every right to be here and is perfectly behaved."

Laura-Jean made a noncommittal noise and fluffed her hair and turned away.

"Your mother mentioned the woman with the Pastor is his wife and she's a friend of yours?"

"Ex-wife." Laura-Jean focused her attention back on Lila. "They divorced a little while ago and I'm just an acquaintance. Not close at all. At least, not to Chastity," Laura-Jean simpered.

"Aha. So, she must've remained friends with her ex if she's at the party talking to him?"

"Chastity has certain issues." Laura-Jean grimaced. "Money unfortunately tends to run through her fingers. She's probably asking for a top-up. Ezekiel has family money. But don't get any ideas." She eyed Lila up and down. "He has options that don't include bakers." Turning her nose up in the air, she prowled toward the whispering couple.

"Poor Ezekiel. Those women stalk him continuously. Especially his ex-wife." A woman in her sixties sidled up next to Lila, her no-nonsense thick-soled shoes squeaking on the floor.

"Laura-Jean mentioned Chastity has issues with money."

"Issues." The woman snorted. "She's a loose cannon with expensive tastes. Poor Ezekiel suffers greatly."

Yet he didn't exactly look like he suffered as Chastity wiggled up next to her ex-husband.

"Now, now, Agnes. No need to be catty. Chastity's officially out of the picture. Gives me a clear run at our distinguished Pastor." A plump, silvery blonde-haired lady elbowed the other woman.

Agnes pursed her thin lips. "It's unbecoming to speak of the head of our church like that." She straightened her already stiffened spine until she resembled a flat ironing board. Wiry hair surrounded her head in an explosion of gray curls.

"Seems like the good old Pastor is leaving a trail of single ladies."

"The Pastor's not interested in such banality as dating. He has more important things to focus on." Agnes tore her gaze away from the fawning Laura-Jean as the younger woman giggled at the Pastor. "Now, excuse me, I should speak to Marcy and wish her a happy birthday." Agnes stomped off in her sensible shoes.

"What a killjoy. She likes the old boy as much as we all do." Elaine winked at Lila. "When you get my age, there's slim pickings in the man department." She tugged her neckline down an inch and sauntered off toward the Pastor's growing fan club.

"Point Muse gets crazier every minute," Lila muttered.

"You're surprised at this?" Es Penne popped up next to Lila. "All the cupcakes, brownies, and lemon slices are laid out and the cake is unboxed and waiting for the birthday girl."

"Good. Now you get to break up the singles' dating group and tell Laura-Jean we're ready to go."

"You should pay me extra for that. Those women

are barracudas when it comes to the Pastor. They might bite me."

"I think the big dragon can take on dentured old women. Now once more into the fray." Lila shoved Es in the group's direction.

The teenage dragon shot Lila a withering glance but complied.

Lila checked on the cake, making sure candles, knife, and lighter were all readily available.

Nash, Lila's black hellhound puppy, deserted his own groupies and sidled up to her, whining and sniffing at the cake.

Tapping the hellhound on his nose, Lila shook her head. "No cake for you. Laura-Jean isn't happy you're here and I think she wanted your dessert besties instead of me. So, no cake for us. We're on our best behavior."

Laura-Jean bustled up, with her mother in tow. "If you're finally ready, I'd like to start."

Lila nodded and stepped back as Laura-Jean clapped her hands for attention.

"Quiet, please." She waited for the noise to die down before speaking again. "Thank you to everyone who turned up to wish my mother a happy birthday. Even the four-legged guests." Laura-Jean frowned at a whining Nash who'd sidled up next to her. Laure

Jean snatched the lighter up and lit the candles. She gestured to her mother to come in close.

With her daughter's help, Marcy blew out all the candles. She handed the knife over to Laura-Jean and grabbed a cupcake, before heading back to her cronies.

Laura-Jean sliced the knife expertly through the multiple layers of mud cake. She withdrew the knife and left it hanging at her side. A large core of lavender icing decorated the tip of one of her red nails. Shrugging, she licked the nail, giggling. Which turned into a sharp squeal as Nash lunged forward and took a large lick of the knife, smearing purple icing over his muzzle.

Laura-Jean dropped the knife on the table. "Bad puppy." She pointed at Lila. "See? What did I say about pets?"

"Oh, my goodness. Is this how parties are conducted in Point Muse?" Chastity strolled up next to Laura-Jean and grimaced at the purple and pink rose-covered cake. "How over the top. Old people really don't have fashionable tastes, do they?"

Laura-Jean shut her mouth and scratched her scalp.

Nash scooted next to Lila and hung his head, scratching at his nose and side.

"I'm extremely sorry. I have no clue what came over him. He's normally very well-behaved." Lila knew exactly what had got into Nash. An obsessive love of sugar. He had no willpower when it came to icing.

"Don't expect a glowing reference from me." Laura-Jean frantically itched her scalp. "What is wrong with my head? It only started itching after I had icing." She glared at Lila.

Nash dropped to the ground and flipped onto his back, trying to scratch.

"Nash?" Lila knelt next to her puppy and ran a hand over his side and nose. Tiny raised bumps had spread over his skin. Lila lifted her hands away from the hellhound and a large clump of fur came with her.

"No." Laura-Jean shrieked and held her hands out to Lila. "What have you done?" Like Nash, large chunks of her auburn hair now lay in the hysterical woman's hands.

"You poisoned her?" Chastity shrieked and shoved people away from the cake. "Don't eat it. It's poisoned."

"Hey. My food is fine," Lila protested.

"Fine? My pride and joy is falling out in my

hands." Laura-Jean shook a handful of her hair at Lila.

Es popped up as Lila sighed. "I called Braun; he should be here any minute."

Lila nodded. "Don't let anyone else eat the cake, just in case."

"That's right, girl. Take the innocent victims away from the poisoned cake." Chastity grabbed Laura-Jean and spun away from Lila.

"Now, dear, I'm sure Ms. Harrow hasn't intentionally poisoned anyone. This is all a mistake." Ezekiel stepped up, a warm fatherly smile in place. "Ms. Harrow worked very hard on Marcy's cake. This is all a misunderstanding."

"Misunderstanding?" Laura-Jean screeched. "This is my beautiful hair." She lurched toward the pastor and collapsed against him, sobbing.

Ezekiel's church groupies closed ranks around the pair and led them off to a quiet corner.

Chastity bared bright white teeth at Lila. "I'll make sure everyone knows what you did. I told Laura-Jean she should've gone with the Devlins and their desserts." She flounced off and joined her hair-challenged friend.

"Making friends, I see." Zach Braun joined Lila.

Lila held up her hands. "I swear this has nothing

to do with me and Elspeth's nowhere to be seen. It isn't Harrow-caused."

Braun patted Lila's back. "I'm sorry but we have to take the food and test it. Because I can guarantee, Laura-Jean will make a complaint. She's always been vain about her hair."

"Take it all. Nothing to do with my bakery. Everyone knows my van is always unlocked. Anyone could have sabotaged my cake." Lila snapped her fingers. "In fact, I saw the Devlins bakery van in the car park when I arrived. They definitely could have done this."

Frowning, Zach gathered the evidence. "Don't jump to conclusions. This could be caused by anything. No need to blame the Devlins."

"We'll see." Lila crossed her arms and matched Braun's frown. She had a bad feeling the hair loss incident was the tip of the iceberg...

THREE

"Fully bald within twenty-four hours. That's a doozy of a hex." Elspeth whistled, looking impressed.

"Could we not applaud the fact my cake stripped the client of all of her hair? It isn't exactly the best advertisement for my business." Lila tapped her short round nails on the table to the tune of the death march.

"Calm down, drama llama. At least Nash is okay."

Lila ran a hand over the back of her slumbering pup. He still had some bare patches but what a difference a day and a potion from Aunt Winifred could make. "Yeah, Aunt Winifred is a potion goddess."

Elspeth sniffed. "I wouldn't go that far, but she does have a light touch for healing potions."

"She needs to, living with Elspeth," Xandie whispered.

"I can hear you, granddaughter. Just because you're a Librarian doesn't mean you can escape my wrath." Elspeth glared at Xandie.

Xandie mimed zipping her lips and remained quiet until Elspeth turned back to spy on the Devlin bakery. As soon as she knew she was safe, Xandie slipped out of her chair, disappearing into the kitchen.

"Anyone know how Laura-Jean's doing?"

"Laura-Jean is considering suing your sub-par establishment." A fuming Laura-Jean stood framed in the bakery doorway. She had a floral hat jammed tight on her head.

Lila shuddered as Chastity Moss loomed like a stiletto-wearing blonde doomsayer behind her hairless friend.

"You'll be lucky to get out of this with your tacky shirt intact," Chastity sneered at Lila. "Laura-Jean's pain and suffering will bankrupt you."

"I did nothing wrong. Braun hasn't even had the results back from my food yet. This is all an assumption. My van wasn't locked. Anyone, including the

Devlins, could have access to my food for sabotage." Lila crossed arms over her chest and glared. She felt bad for the snooty Laura-Jean. Losing your pride and joy was tough but until evidence to the contrary presented itself, she wasn't admitting liability to anyone. "You should see our Aunt Winifred. Her potions worked wonders on Nash."

Nash stood and gently shook himself. Half a dozen bare patches showed on one side, but the majority had thickened and grown over already.

"Poor kid. Baldness ain't a joke." The pug shoved a small cupcake with blue icing at Nash. "Never say I don't share in the face of tragedy. Lap it up while you can."

Nash shrunk away from the cupcake, shaking his head.

Gasping, Colin shook his head. "Scared of cake. What a way to go. Nash. Buddy. Don't go toward the light."

Chastity rolled her eyes, shoving her friend out of the way. She strolled into the bakery. "What a dump. Seriously? The homey look went out years ago. You need more class, like that dessert place across the road. It looks amazing."

Red film covered Lila's eyes and she opened her mouth to reply but someone else got there before her.

"And you'd know all about class, Chastity Moss. Wouldn't you?" Agnes Bartholomew stepped up to the counter, a few of her church choir cronies crowded in behind her.

Raising over-picked eyebrows, Chastity sneered at the older woman. "More than you, Agnes. Stagnating here in Point Muse, mooning over my husband. Pathetic really."

Agnes's hard brown eyes flashed. "Ex-husband! And he's a much-loved resident of Point Muse. You are not. You're a blow-in looking for a cash grab just like those dessert sinners across the road." Agnes nodded at Lila's competition across the road.

"Why you…" Chastity lurched forward, surprising a squeak out of her friend.

"I think it's time you ladies left. Laura-Jean, you should visit my daughter. She'll fix you up. Sadly, she can't do anything about Chastity's mouth or character." Elspeth entered from the back of the bakery, a diminutive dictator in a lavender jogging suit with matching purple mohawk wig. Shadows rippled around her then thickened and surged toward the stiletto-shod blonde.

Chastity swallowed heavily and took a tiny step back, bumping into her friend.

Laura-Jean grabbed the back of Chastity's shirt.

"Don't mess with the wicked witch. Time to leave." Laura-Jean raised her voice. "Thank you, Elspeth. I'll go there right now and see Winifred." She kept tugging on Chastity's shirt until the duo cleared the bakery.

Lila sagged in her seat, the weight of her customers' stares weighing her shoulders down. She hunched over, avoiding everyone's gaze. Sooner rather than later, the rest of her customers would begin to agree with Chastity. Her bakery would lose business, even before the dessert bakery opened.

"Such a vulgar woman." Agnes and her choir cronies stood around Lila's table. Each one held a cake box. "Honestly, everything out of her mouth is a lie." Agnes juggled her cake box. "Obviously the church committee has no issues with your food at all."

Lila mustered a weak smile. "Thanks, Agnes. I appreciate your support."

"Nonsense. Only speaking the truth. Something that woman wouldn't know about."

"I take it you don't like Chastity?"

Agnes snorted. "I don't like the fact she keeps popping back into Pastor Moss's life and bank accounts. When her latest scheme fails, she turns up like a bad penny looking for a handout. It's very stressful for poor Pastor Moss."

"Tell the truth, Agnes Bartholomew. You can't stand her because she is Ezekiel's ex-wife." Elaine Purdy leaned on Lila's table and smirked.

"She's as greedy as Laura-Jean is prideful about her appearance. Both are a disgrace to the church community."

Elaine rolled her eyes. "You're a self-righteous gossip, Agnes." Standing, Elaine smoothed down her form-fitting dress. "Ciao, churchies. I have to hurry and help our Ezekiel set up for the church meeting." She blew a kiss to Agnes and hurried out.

"Man, this place is like a train station. Gossip in and out regularly." Colin scratched his head with a paw. "I feel the need for sustenance, Queen of my life."

Elspeth hurried over from her perch at the window and scooped up the pug. "Can't have my sweetie expiring from hunger. Let's see what Hester has fresh out of the oven." Ignoring the rest of the bakery, Elspeth ambled into the kitchen.

One of the ladies in Agnes's group elbowed the older woman and pointed to her watch.

Agnes waved the other ladies on. "I'll be with you in a moment." Waiting for the ladies to leave,

Agnes lowered her voice. "I'm sure you're concerned about the impact of that dessert place."

"They aren't even open yet." Xandie popped out of the kitchen with a plate of savory biscuits. She dumped them in front of Lila. "Hester says eat up; you're wasting away."

"Nevertheless," Agnes ignored Xandie, "I've heard things about that family. You need to watch your back, Lila Harrow." Agnes paused for a moment as if searching for the right words. "I also heard the Devlin family employs less than ethical means to run their competitors out of business."

"I guess we'll see." Lila forced a smile to her face. It made her feel slightly yucky trading in gossip. Even if it was about those dessert wenches.

"Unfortunately, I think you will." Agnes leaned in close. "If you want more information, I hear Portland was the last port of call for the family. Apparently, the matriarch is quite nefarious." Agnes nodded meaningfully at Lila before straightening and speaking in a normal tone of voice. "Now the reason I wanted to speak to you is that the church has quite a few activities coming up that will need catering. I think you should apply."

"Doesn't Marcie do all the catering for any

church activities?" Lila loved cooking but Marcie took baking to a whole new level.

"Poor Marcie is having an arthritis flare-up. She needs someone to take over momentarily. Since the church has the upcoming dance and church meeting which both need catering, I think you would be perfect."

The old girl could be right. With Marcie out of the running, getting some church gigs might help her over her current slump. "Thanks, Agnes. I'll apply. It can't hurt, can it?"

Agnes beamed at Lila. "That's the spirit, Harrow. And the farmers' market is on tomorrow too. Best you show your wares and out-maneuver those dessert sinners. Show them what Point Muse residents can do."

"I'll be there, Agnes."

With a stiff nod, Agnes stomped outside to her milling group of churchgoers.

Two women broke off from the group and opened the bakery door. "We heard about what happened at the home. So sad for that poor woman losing her hair." Ruby Devlin patted her long curly black tresses in sympathy.

Rose, her twin, clicked her tongue. "At least it

wasn't more serious. We've all heard about Point Muse's reputation for body count."

Great, the smirking competition had arrived. "Like I told Chastity, until the Police Chief gets back to me with test results, we have no clue what poisoned Laura-Jean." Lila shot a pointed look at the twins. "Didn't I see your van in the car park? Maybe you saw something?"

Ruby looked worried at Lila's words. "Oh gosh, Zachy already asked us questions. We saw nothing out of the ordinary."

"So why were you there anyway?"

"We were just driving around, familiarizing ourselves with Point Muse, that's all." Rose beamed at Lila.

"Uh huh." She believed that just as much as when Elspeth fed her a lie.

Leaning against the counter, Ruby winked. "I heard there's a farmers' market tomorrow. Sister and I thought we'd have a little pop-up stall. Get Point Muse used to our food. Isn't that a great idea?"

"Peachy."

Rose glanced around the bakery. "Quiet in here. Is the lunchtime rush finished already?"

And there was the passive-aggressive attack. Why were the men never around to see that? "Just a normal pause, it'll pick up. Besides, I have a few baking opportunities coming up. I'm going to be pretty busy."

"I heard about the church dance and the dinner." Ruby widened her eyes, looking innocent. "Elaine made a point of telling us outside. So wonderful that Point Muse has these activities that can support healthy competition, isn't it?"

The kitchen door slammed open, and Elspeth strutted out. "Looks like the bad pennies have turned up. Lock your food and your men up. The Devlins will poison both."

Xandie grabbed the plate of savory biscuits from the table and strode into Lila's office. "Just avoiding the Elspeth carnage. Carry on," she yelled over her shoulder, surprising a hard-at-work Matthew Grim.

Ruby lost her smile, her face hardening. "That's the rest of the family. We're just here to make sinful desserts."

Elspeth cackled, shadows weaved in and out around the tables and chairs, pulling close to the twins.

Both women took a measured step back, running into Zach Braun. He placed his hands on both women's shoulders and steadied them. "Now, Elspeth. We've talked about you intimidating innocent Point Muse residents with your shadows. Lock it down, Harrow."

Grunting, Elspeth snapped fingers and the shadows leached back into her. "Innocence is in the eye of the beholder, and this beholder spies no good."

"As long as you keep your shadows to yourself, I don't care what you spy." Braun frowned and turned to Lila. "We need to speak about those test results when you have some free time, Ms. Harrow."

Name-calling from law enforcement was never a good thing. "Whenever you have some spare time, Chief Braun." Lila pointedly stared at his hand on the women's shoulders.

"I'll walk the Devlins back to the bakery. But when I'm finished, you and I will talk."

"What a surprise. A strong man turned weak-willed by the flutter of Devlin eyelashes." Elspeth sneered at the bear shifter as he retreated out of the bakery with the women.

Xandie poked her head out of the office, Matthew standing next to her. "Coast clear yet?"

"It is, thanks to your not-so sweetie." Elspeth spun and glared at Xandie.

"Hey? What did I do?"

"Rein the shifter in, Librarian. He's going to get burned by those bakery wenches and I, for one, won't be leaping to his rescue." Elspeth huffed and stormed out, blue mohawk waving, in a rush to leave.

"Braun apparently needs to talk to me about my food's test results, but he had to walk his little darlings back to the bakery first." Lila stared at her scratched tabletop morosely.

"That bear shifter. Cut his honeybuns. Do you hear me, Lila Harrow? No more," Xandie cursed.

Matthew winced and stepped away from Xandie. "I think the whole of Point Muse heard you."

"Since Braun needs to talk to me, I guess my food came back positive for some kind of poison or hex."

Grim strolled closer. "Don't jump to conclusions."

"Jump to conclusions?" Her depression forgotten, Lila jumped up and thumped a finger in the middle of her boyfriend's chest. "My food is hex free, it's those dessert witches he should be looking at. Maybe start with the mysterious pantry stocked with herbs that you wouldn't normally see in a dessert recipe. How about that?" Lila panted as she delivered her diatribe.

The reaper raised an eyebrow at her dramatics. "Maybe he's willing to give them the benefit of the doubt until he sees evidence to prove otherwise."

"Please." Lila rolled her eyes. "Maybe he and you were both swayed by long eyelashes."

Matthew shook his head, a disappointed expression on his face. "Quit whining and find proof of their wrongdoing and that goes for Elspeth too." He strode back to the office and shut the door with a decisive bang.

"Fine, I will," Lila hollered back.

If it were the last thing she did, both flirty witches were going down... She just had to find proof.

Easier said than done.

FOUR

"Ah, the chirping birds, stalls overlaid with fresh goods and the scent of blood in the water." Elspeth grinned, enjoying the farmers' market. "It's my kind of place."

"As long as there's a chance of mayhem, you'll be lurking," Lila mocked her grandmother while she set out brightly colored iced cupcakes.

"That's why Gran's hovering. She wants to see the baked good fireworks." Es Penne, teenage dragon, handed a container full of bright pink strawberry slices to Lila.

"One can't admire chaos in Point Muse anymore?" Marjorie Penne, matriarch of the Pendrakon clan, grandmother to Es Penne and poker crony of Elspeth's, winked at Lila.

The elderly dragon could sometimes be a calming influence on Elspeth, although those times were few and far between lately. Tall and angular, the dragon had a no-nonsense silver bob and a stern gaze, but her teenage granddaughter proved she was really a marshmallow. "Just keep an eye on Elspeth. She's already hair-trigger and Braun's itching to lock her up before she hurts his darlings." Lila rolled her eyes and refused to look at the stall the Devlins had set up directly opposite her.

Marjorie saluted Lila, then linked her arm through Elspeth's emerald-green, velour-covered arm. "Will do, Lila." The two older women strolled off cackling.

"You truly trust my grandmother to keep an eye on yours?" Es shook her long black hair. "You've been dipping into your stash of chocolate."

"As long as she's away from me, I don't care... Well, as long as no bodies turn up, I mean," Lila amended.

"With mother, there is always a body or two in her wake." Amelia Harrow and Shade, Hades' right-hand man, strolled up to Lila's stall.

Her parents had renewed their vows a little while ago. After Hades agreed to her father spending more time in Point Muse, Lila's mother, Amelia, had finally come clean and admitted they'd never broken up, but instead, hid their relationship from Lila to make it easy on her when he had to leave to deal with Hades' business. "Marjorie promised she'd look after Elspeth."

Amelia arched an eyebrow and narrowed her eyes at her daughter. Tall and skinny with the same colored eyes as the rest of the Harrow women, Lila's mother was the town's vet and animal empath. No-nonsense to a fault, she balanced out Shade's more flamboyant tendencies. *Speaking of her father...*

Shade twitched his shoulders and reached out a hand furtively, aiming for a pink-colored slice.

"Dad? You can ask me for a slice, you know."

Lila's father snapped his hand back to his side with a shame-faced grin. "Keeping my hand in. Can't lose my edge now I live in Point Muse permanently." He waggled thick silver eyebrows at Lila.

"Here." She shoved a napkin and a strawberry slice at her father. "Go forth and munch, old man."

"Thanks, dear." Shade snatched the slice from his daughter and took a large bite. Rolling his eyes, he mumbled something around his mouthful.

Amelia clapped her husband on the back. "What have I told you? Don't speak with a full mouth."

Shrugging, Shade swallowed. "I need to clear room for the rest."

"Rest?"

Lila's father nodded at the farmers' market. "I intend to graze through all this amazing spread, barring any Elspeth-caused mayhem."

"No point hoping for that," Amelia muttered, then shoved her husband toward the Rotunda and the church choir. "Let's get some culture before you fill your stomach and start moaning about a tummy ache." Waving goodbye, the couple wound their way through the crowd.

"It's a good turnout today." Lila's Aunt Winifred nodded, satisfied. "I should sell a few of my perfumed soaps and lotions. I have a new blend of lavender and lime I want to try on my customers."

Winifred had wrangled a spot next to Lila. She theorized that if she had a spot next to a popular food stall, she could siphon the overflowing customers over to her face creams and soaps. "Yeah, I just wish everyone would stop staring at me, wondering who I'll poison next."

"You can't help it. If a Harrow's in residence, the probability of a body rises by fifty percent." Holly wandered up, munching on a fresh apple with Xandie trailing behind her, silent.

"What's wrong with our pouty cousin?"

"Braun dumped her to help carry the Devlins' devilish baked goods. She's sulking."

Xandie drew to a halt next to Lila's stall. "Pouting is for Elspeth when she doesn't get her way. I am announcing my displeasure at Braun's priorities. That's all." Xandie turned around and glared across the way at the dessert bakery stall.

"Yep. I guessed it was something like that." Lila handed Xandie a blue-iced cupcake. "Have this. It's my new concoction. *Beat the Blues* coconut and lime cupcake. Should make you feel better." At least she could still count on her baking to make customers feel good. As long as someone didn't sabotage her food. Any Harrow witchy gifts she had were poured into her baked goods. She loved the buzz and happy feelings she could impart to her customers through her baking. "Come to think of it, maybe I should have a cupcake myself." Lila grabbed one of her blue cupcakes and munched, sighing contentedly when the lime flavor exploded on her tongue.

"Lila, dear, I'm glad you took my advice and decided to open a stall at the farmers' market. You need to be seen out and about. Put all those nasty rumors to bed." Agnes smiled at Lila before handing her some pamphlets. "It's a faint hope to expect your grandmother to honor us with her presence, but there's always a chance she might turn up to a service or a church activity."

"When the underworld freezes over," Xandie muttered.

"Thanks, Agnes. I'll make sure she gets it." Lila tucked away the pamphlets. "I also decided to apply for the catering for the dance and the church meeting. Hopefully, whoever makes the decision will ignore the hair loss issue."

Agnes frowned. "No way is that your fault. I heard those Devlins were spotted outside the retirement home. I have no doubt at all that they're behind the poisoning."

"Can I quote you on that, Agnes?" Percy Hague, editor and lone reporter for the Point Muse chronicles, strolled up, camera hanging around his neck.

Stiffening, Agnes glared at the newshound. "No, you may not, Mr. Hague. I suggest you focus on taking pictures of the goods and services offered at the market instead of focusing on rumor and innuendo." Agnes nodded to Lila and stomped off toward the warbling church choir.

Percy shuddered. "That woman gives me the heebies."

Holly giggled. "Is that special reporter language?"

"More like normal Point Muse language." Percy eyed Lila's stall. "Everything looks delicious, Lila. What do you recommend?"

"Not afraid of sudden hair loss?"

"I think I'll risk it."

"I'm happy to reward your bravery." Lila winked and placed a couple of pieces of her fudge slice onto a napkin. "You're in such a good mood, I think you can taste my *Frolicking Fudge* slice."

"Taken with grateful thanks. But while I'm here, I don't suppose you want to comment on the hair loss incident at the retirement home by any chance?" Percy adjusted his black rimmed glasses and stared at Lila.

"Nope. All I can say is I had nothing to do with it and that it was more than likely sabotage."

"I'm assuming you're alluding to the mysterious Devlin twins?"

"I have no clue who the perpetrators were, but I will track them down." Lila flashed a tight grin at Percy. The newshound was a nice guy who'd helped them before, but she wasn't in the mood to be misquoted by Point Muse's local newspaper.

"You're a Harrow, I would expect no less. I think

I might check these devilish Devlins out myself." With a salute, Percy wandered across to the twins.

Xandie sidled up next to Lila. Both women stared at the intrepid newshound as he leaned against the dessert bakery stall and chatted. "What is it about those two women?" Ruby fluttered eyelashes at the reporter, while Rose giggled with one hand over her mouth. "At least Grim and Braun aren't dancing attendance for once."

"I beg to differ." Xandie pointed to a lumbering bear shifter coming up behind the twins, loaded down with boxes.

"Whoops, sorry." Lila grimaced.

"I could take them out. Wouldn't take much." Miranda, Xandie's mom and Lila's aunt and ex-black ops, enveloped both girls in a warm hug.

Xandie snickered, her earlier griping forgotten. "Thanks, Mom. You're always there when I need you."

The twinkle in Miranda's eyes dimmed a little. "I am now. Anything you need, sweet pea, I've got your back."

Lila extricated herself from the hug and patted her aunt on the back. "Thanks for the offer, Miranda. We'll keep it in mind."

Miranda released Xandie from her hug and

winked. "Just let me know. I'm off to see what mayhem Elspeth's caused." Xandie's mother disappeared into the crowd.

"I love the fact your mother can offer to dispose of someone then casually wander off."

"It's a skill." Xandie grimaced. "I hesitate to add more weight to your shoulders, but the Devlins are getting quite a crowd at their stall."

"Yeah." Lila sighed. At least her hellhound wasn't here to desert her for the devilish twins. Hades had decided to take the hellhound home to his mother, Cerberus, for an overnight visit.

"Don't sweat it, sweet cheeks. I can help with that." Colin the pug scooted out from underneath Lila's stall and advanced straight toward the twins' stall.

"Did you know he was under there?"

"I did notice a few cupcakes disappeared, but I thought Elspeth had stolen some."

"Geronimo." Colin's warbled warning was cut off as one of the twins shoved a decadent black forest gateaux in his mouth.

"I might diss the twins, but honestly, that move was smooth," Lila admitted.

"Yep." Xandie sighed. "Those two definitely have moves."

Lila echoed Xandie's sigh and scanned the farmers' market. The Devlins had a crowd, but another one had gathered around the rotunda, listening to the church choir too.

"I don't care who you are, Horace Painter. I'm in charge of handing out the pamphlets." Agnes's voice rose above the noise of the market.

Lila searched until she saw the woman standing a few stalls away with a short man burdened with bushy gray hair and a large barrel chest.

"You're a dried-up old prune, Agnes. If I remember correctly, it's Elaine's turn to hand out the pamphlets. Isn't that right, Elaine?"

Elaine Purdy simpered next to Horace. "Why, I do believe you're right." She snatched the pamphlets away from Agnes. "Point Muse needs all the religious help it can get. I mean, look at what happened at the retirement home? That poor woman losing her pride, her beautiful hair." Elaine shuddered in sympathy.

Agnes glared at the couple. "Nothing but an accident, but maybe Laura-Jean shouldn't have been so prideful. It *is* a sin."

"Now, now. Please, we're all friends here. Harsh words aren't needed." Ezekiel Moss, the Pastor, split the pamphlets up and gave a portion to each of them.

He held a hand for his churchgoers to wait and rushed over to Lila. "Some cupcakes, Lila? I need to soothe some flaring tempers."

Smiling, Lila handed over a plastic tray of *Calm Down* coconut slices. "Instead of a cupcake, try these. They should work."

Ezekiel nodded and headed back, only to be waylaid by some energetic parishioners. He stopped in front of the still-warring trio. "Now, let's all calm down. Share this wonderful food Lila's provided." He held up the tray of slices.

Elaine slid an arm around the pastor's waist and laid her head against his arm. "What a wonderful idea, Ezekiel."

Horace stepped forward, dislodging Elaine from her limpet hold on the pastor's arm. "I haven't got time for this nonsense. I've got a job to do." He glared at Elaine and stomped off, shoving pamphlets in people's faces.

Agnes pasted a tight-lipped smile firmly on her face. "I think that's a lovely idea. I haven't tried any of Lila's delicious food yet." She reached out a hand, but Elaine beat her to it, snatching a piece out of Agnes's reach.

"What a good idea. I'll just have this piece." Elaine took a large bite and swallowed. She smiled victoriously at Agnes, but the smile suddenly flickered as she coughed into her hand. "Must have had a burnt bit on the slice. Tasted quite bitter." She coughed again and gripped her throat. Her eyes bulged and her tongue hung out of the corner of the mouth, a startling bright green color.

"Elaine? Are you okay?" Ezekiel dropped the slice tray on the ground as he and Agnes crowded around the coughing woman.

She gripped her throat tighter. The noises coming from Elaine now sounded like a hoarse frog. She dropped to her knees, her face drained of color, before she toppled over and lay still on the ground.

The crowd drew away from the woman and stared accusingly at Lila's stall.

"Again?" Lila moaned and hid behind Xandie's shoulder for a moment before popping back up. "Where's Elspeth?"

"Don't worry about Elspeth. Watch your reaper in action."

Matthew Grim, Point Muse's reaper at large, and Lila's boyfriend, moved through the crowd with Braun following.

The two men knelt next to Elaine. Braun checked for a pulse but shook his head.

Nodding to something Braun said, the reaper

drew his pen-sized scythe out of his pocket and placed the tip against the dead woman's forehead. A warm yellow glow emanated from the scythe. The same glow covered Elaine's body until it slowly dissipated.

"Told you, where the Devlins go, so does the body count." Elspeth popped up next to Lila and sniffed. "That Elaine. Cat on a hot tin roof whenever she got near that Ezekiel. Talk about lusting after religion."

Lila glared at her grandmother. "Tell me you didn't have anything to do with that poor woman's death?"

"Please, I'm way more subtle than..." Elspeth trailed off. Her face flamed red, and then paled.

"You okay, Elspeth? You look like you saw a ghost."

Elspeth bared her teeth. "Worse than that."

"My, my. Elspeth, how wonderful you look in your..." A tiny, older woman with long curly black hair with silver streaks and a flowing dress stopped at Lila's stall. "Did you match your green wig to your jogging suit? How precious." The older woman trilled a melodious laugh that filled the quiet park and the farmers' market.

"Delilah Devlin. The devil herself," Elspeth spat

the woman's name. "I thought the bad penny would turn up sooner rather than later."

"Why, Elspeth Harrow, you say the nicest things." Delilah beamed. "I'm just here to support my granddaughters. Now, excuse me, I simply must meet up with them. Tootles." She waggled her ring-encrusted fingers at Elspeth and strutted off.

"You want a suspect? Look no further than that woman." Elspeth gnashed her teeth. "I knew the Devlins were behind the poisoning. The Harrows need to plan our next course of action."

"We need to do something more than that." They had to track down a murderer. *Because knowing Point Muse, the odds were not in favor of a natural death…*

FIVE

"I'm a pariah. And in Point Muse that says something." Lila lowered her head behind the menu.

"That's Elspeth's paranoia talking." Matthew grabbed Lila's menu and dumped it on the table. "You don't need the menu anyway. You always get the same thing every time we come here."

Lila shrugged. "What can I say? Rose's lobster rolls are to die for." She froze for a moment. "I don't mean that literally. You hear me, fate? Not literally."

"I think you need to lower your sugar intake. You're getting a little crazy." Matthew reached out a hand and toyed with Lila's clenched fist. "We're having a nice dinner at Mayweather Inn. We're in a secluded corner and candlelight is flickering. Just relax."

Sagging in her chair, she let her fist unclench under Matthew's calloused hand. "Someone tastes my icing and loses her hair. Another eats my slice and chokes to death. We both know what's going on. It's Point Muse. This is the beginning of the body count... And everyone thinks my food is killing people."

"It will work it out. Braun knows you'd never hurt anyone." Matthew stroked a finger over Lila's now flattened hand. "You're not Elspeth. No one thinks you're capable of murder. Trust me, Braun's busy hunting the real killer down."

Lila snorted. "Zach Braun's busy with his second job of renovating. Pretty soon, Xandie will ask Elspeth to turn him into a hammer if he doesn't stop spending every waking moment with the Devlin twins."

"He's trying to help get the apartment ready for their grandmother. Besides, he feels sorry for them after all the rumors Elspeth's been spreading."

Lila slid her hand out from under Matthew's and glared at the reaper. "Not rumors. First-hand accounts. Elspeth has tangled with Delilah before. And now Delilah's been suspiciously quiet in the last twenty-four hours since the farmers' market. Elspeth's expecting a worst-case scenario."

"That's between those two. Her granddaughters don't deserve the whole town to be turned against them." The reaper frowned. "I know you're worried about your business, but there's room in Point Muse for two bakeries."

Seriously, the reaper was completely blind. "Maybe if you and Braun didn't run off to help the twins every five minutes, I wouldn't be wound so tight." She glowered at her boyfriend. Could he honestly not see the flirtatious manipulation?

Matthew cleared his throat. "You know you have nothing to worry about."

Lila opened her mouth, but Matthew spoke over her, in a rush to get his words out. "I have to take a trip to Portland to deposit some souls and to get an upgrade on my scythe. I thought you might want to tag along with me. Meet the rest of my family?"

"Say what?" Lila squeaked the words out. He wanted her to meet his family? She'd met Ed, his father, and spoken to his mother on the phone, but meeting his siblings as well? Lila grabbed a glass of water and chugged a large mouthful, taking her time swallowing to think of a polite reply.

"You don't want to?" Hurt colored Matthew's words.

"Of course, I do. It's... I..." Lila blurted out, her

measured response forgotten. She stumbled to a halt. She struggled to put into words her anxiety at meeting his family, which seemed selfish since he'd met all of hers.

Understanding dawned on Matthew's face. "You're freaked out at meeting them?"

Flinging her hands up, Lila narrowly missed knocking over her drink. "I'm a Harrow. A body count follows us wherever we go. And don't even mention Elspeth," Lila wailed. "Maybe you *should* date the devilish Devlins."

Matthew bit back a laugh. "My father loves Elspeth, and my mother regularly rings your grandmother for mayhem updates. Trust me, you'll fit right in with Grim Inc."

"I'll think about it." Lila offered a weak smile and fought the urge to wipe sweat away from her forehead. Meeting his family was a big step, but if she didn't take that step, the Devlin twins waited in the wings. She might have to Harrow up and meet his family.

"Matthew Grim, what a pleasure to see you in my establishment." Rose Mayweather, descendant of Aphrodite, the goddess of love, and a fifties style housewife wannabe, bustled over and ran a hand over Matthew's shoulders.

What was it with Point Muse women and touching the reaper?

"Hi, Rose, thanks for fitting us in."

Turning a snort into a cough, Lila looked around the dining room. A total of six customers filled the large dining room.

Matthew shoved his foot against Lila's in warning.

Lila nodded and followed her boyfriend's lead. "Thanks. We appreciate getting away for some quiet time."

Rose smoothed a hand over her bouffant blonde locks. "No trouble for our local reaper. Plus, I knew you'd need some time to yourself, Lila. After everything that's happened, I mean."

Great, things were bad if even the town's most ardent Harrow-hater felt bad for her. Lila nodded but forced her tongue to be still.

"In fact," Rose leant toward them, her eyes darting to Lila, "That woman is staying here, you know. She spends a lot of time in the bar."

Matthew's phone rang, and he excused himself to answer it.

Focusing on Rose, Lila tried not to listen to Matthew's one-sided phone call.

"You need to fight for your man, sweetie." Rose

sympathetically patted Lila's hand. "That Delilah is bad news for the love business, not to mention every couple in Point Muse."

"Ah huh." Lila shot a quick glance over at Matthew, who seemed engrossed in a secret phone call.

Rose dropped into Matthew's discarded seat. "I know the Harrows and I'm not on overly cordial terms, but that Delilah Devlin plays fast and loose with love, life, and flirting. Plus, she's rowdy and constantly mouthing off about Elspeth. I do *not* want a war with your grandmother. My Inn couldn't withstand that level of battle." Rose sat back and slapped a hand on the table. "So, fight for that man, distract Elspeth, and get that woman out of my inn." Rose jumped up with a wide fake smile as Matthew strode to the table. "My goodness, what a strange, pained look on your face, Matthew. It must be Harrow-related." Beaming, Rose minced away after giving Lila a knowing glance.

"Tell me your phone call didn't involve another body or Elspeth?"

"Not this time." Matthew cleared his throat. "That was Braun. Apparently, the twins need to speak to their grandmother urgently. He's asked me to pick her up from the bar and drop her at their bakery."

"After our date, you mean."

"Seems they need to see her as soon as possible. We'll have to cut our date short. I'm sorry, Lila. I swear I'll make it up to you."

"I guess it's a good thing we hadn't ordered then." Lila grabbed a drink of water and drained it. *She could do this.* She could be the bigger Harrow. Prove she trusted her boyfriend... *Even if it killed her.* Standing, Lila gestured to Matthew. "Lead the way, Grim."

Letting out a deep breath, Matthew strode toward the noisy bar and opened the door for Lila.

Stepping inside, Lila blinked as the noise of raucous partiers washed over her. And holding court at the bar, surrounded by a bevy of bearded beauties, Delilah Devlin. "Pry Elspeth's nemesis away from her admirers but watch out for claws. I bet she bites too," Lila couldn't help but sneer. There was only so much a Harrow could take.

The twins' grandmother had dressed in a tight pair of black jeans, high-heeled boots, and flowing purple top. Half a dozen jangling bracelets decorated one arm and her silver-streaked black hair lay trussed up on top of the head in a loose bun. Bright red lipstick completed the femme fatale image.

"Is he ready to lose a limb?" Melody Braun, Zach's little sister, stomped up to Lila. "Those men around her don't want any more competition, including my own blind date," Melody growled, sounding more like a wolf, than a bear shifter.

"*We* were on a date too but, apparently, the Devlins' grandmother is needed urgently back at Devilish Desserts." Lila bared her teeth. "I'm being understanding. Can you tell?"

"Definitely." Melody nodded. "Can you tell I understand about being deserted by my date?" The bear shifter's claws lengthened as she picked at her blush pink nail polish.

"We're both very understanding... And now I have to share a car with Elspeth's nemesis. My date night is complete."

Matthew shoved his way through Delilah's groupies and whispered in her ear. One of her admirers placed a hand on the reaper's shoulder and shoved, causing Matthew to back up a step. Delilah laid her head back and roared with laughter.

"I drove tonight in case my date was a dud. How about I give you a lift back and we order pizza?" Melody said.

Matthew shoved the man back and towed a giggling Delilah over to Lila.

Without removing her gaze from the devilish Delilah, Lila nodded. "You know what? I think pizza sounds great."

"It's a date."

Both women fell silent as the femme fatale stopped in front of them.

"Those amber eyes advertise your Harrowness." Delilah clicked fingers. "You're the little baker with the cutie pie puppy, aren't you?"

Matthew winced. "This is my girlfriend, Lila Harrow."

"Of course you are. How can I forget that, and you're Elspeth's eldest granddaughter?"

"That's me. I hear the twins need to speak to you urgently. I'm so glad Matthew's here to help." Lila's smile was saccharine-sweet but must've had a savage edge as the reaper refused to meet her gaze.

"Those girls." Delilah tittered. "Can't make a move without me. It's a good thing I have Matthew here." The twins' grandmother squeezed the reaper's arm. "Such a strong boy." Delilah winked.

"That he is," Lila agreed. "Tonight's worked out quite well. Melody here needs to have some girl time. She can take me home and we'll order pizza. So, your good boy has even more time to spend with you and your granddaughters." Lila smirked at wide-eyed Matthew. "I'm sure Matthew has an amazing idea for another date to top this one. At least, he'd better." Lila winked and turned her back on her boyfriend, stomping off toward the Mayweather Inn's entrance.

Melody giggled. "The expression on his face, so funny. Now he's gonna sweat until he comes up with something epic for a date. Classic revenge."

"I'm all about revenge."

She was Elspeth Harrow's granddaughter after all.

Lila bit into the triple cheese and pepperoni slice and sighed. "I think this pizza might be better than Rose's lobster roll."

"Anything is better than your blind date leaving you for a woman old enough to be your grandmother."

"It's the reason Elspeth can't stand Delilah. Mind you, she doesn't like many people, anyway."

Melody tossed her crust back into the pizza box. "Mom says if Elspeth's slapped on the war paint, you need to get to the bomb shelter asap."

"She's not wrong. And now with Delilah moving into town, it might be time to evacuate Point Muse," Lila joked, but a smidgen of her agreed with the sentiment. Elspeth was gearing up for a fight and no one wanted to be in the fallout zone when the war began.

"Speaking of the Devlins... Zach let it slip the twins have moved into Bertie Boxwoods' old place on the edge of town. Apparently, Delilah wasn't impressed with the two-bedroom accommodation. That's why they're fixing up the apartment for her."

Lila arched an eyebrow. "And I need to know this why?"

Melody winked at Lila. "Just in case someone's house needs searching, or incriminating evidence needs planting."

"My goodness, Deputy Braun. I'm shocked at your suggestion." Lila ruined her serious words with the snicker that slipped out.

"We Point Museians have to stick together."

Without warning, the door to Lila's apartment flung open. Xandie stood framed in the doorway for a moment then slapped a hand over the light switch and plunged the apartment into shadow.

"Why are we now eating pizza in the dark?" Lila enquired.

"Because we're on a mission. Pizza is just a side bonus." Xandie cursed as she walked in to the sofa.

"Wouldn't have happened if you'd left the light on," Lila mocked her cousin.

Melody tapped the light on her phone, illuminating a riled-up Xandie in its meager light.

"What's got you worked up?"

"Braun," Xandie hissed. "Cut our date short... *Again*. It's the Devlins' fault."

Melody and Lila snorted together and toasted Xandie with their margaritas.

"Join the dateless because of the Devlins' club, cuz."

"Not for long." Xandie waved a pair of green binoculars in the air. "I'm here to dig up dirt. These are gonna do that, they even have a night vision setting. Perfect for spying out apartment windows at night." She propped herself up on the floor in front of the window that faced the Devlins' bakery. She eased her head up over the windowsill and settled the binoculars against her face. "Settle in, girls. We have a night of devilish Devlin stalking."

And this is what having a nemesis had driven all three girls to. Snooping with binoculars.

How the Harrows had fallen...

SIX

"Who knew someone could overdose on pizza." Lila rubbed her head and moaned.

"Carb overload is no joke. Neither are the margaritas we consumed." Xandie adjusted her over-large black sunglasses.

Lila slid behind her bakery counter and carefully made herself a strong black coffee. "I regret nothing... Except maybe that midnight raid into Grim's apartment while we were covered in green make-up."

Xandie winced. "I forgot that. Did I really scream tally-ho and take his sock drawer hostage?"

"I have no recollection of our shenanigans last night that I will admit to... Except I have a foggy memory of waxing someone." Lila squinted. "Really hope I didn't attack my hellhound."

"Nash hid under your bed when the wax came out. I should have too." Melody Braun, bear shifter and deputy, slunk into Lila's bakery.

"Are you undercover?" Lila pointed to the black beanie snugged firmly over Melody's head.

The bear shifter pulled the beanie further down. "No, just regretting margaritas and thanking the shifter gods that I'm a hirsute woman whose hair grows quickly."

"Huh?" Lila looked at Xandie, confused.

Leaning in close, Melody pushed the beanie up.

Lila reared back and gasped, hands over her mouth.

Xandie moved her sunglasses to the top of her head and squinted at Melody. "I guess we waxed your eyebrows completely off instead of attacking Nash?"

"It was a close thing. He threatened us with hell fire and then hid under the bed. Apparently, my eyebrows were the next best waxing thing." Melody shifted the beanie back over her hairless brows.

"I am so sorry, Melody," Lila found her voice. "Waxing implements will now be exterminated with extreme prejudice as will margarita mix." She needed to knock off the combination of pizza and alcohol.

Melody shrugged. "I'm a bear shifter. By tomorrow, I'll be back to normal. The night was still better than my aborted blind date would've been."

"You dames rocked out last night." Colin strutted into the bakery. "The pup's in the kitchen, wolfing down hot biscuits that grumpy Brownie baked to soothe his wax trauma. Keeps rambling about no hair."

"I have no recollection and will deny everything. I blame the Devlins and our aborted dates." Lila choked the last of her coffee down and gingerly opened her eyes wide. "I am ready to be an adult now."

"Oh dear, I'm so sorry we disrupted your romantic plans last night." Delilah Devlin strolled in with a woolly animal walking next to her.

"What is that?" Lila pointed a trembling finger at the four-legged monster keeping pace with the devilish Delilah.

The twins' grandmother bent over and smothered the head of the animal in kisses. "This is my Kali. She arrived this morning from Portland. Isn't she perfect?" Delilah cooed to the animal.

"What is she?" Why name a pet the size of a small pony with a ridiculously fuzzy face, paws, and tail, the name of the goddess of time, doomsday, and death.

Delilah frowned. "Kali is a standard poodle and my guard dog. She's perfect."

"You said it." Colin strutted in front of Kali and posed, puffing out his chest. "How goes it, doll face?" The pug winked at the poodle. "I feel a love connection coming on. I got a cupcake with your name on it. What do you say about a doggy date, sweetheart?"

The poodle bared her fangs and growled low her throat.

"Hey." Colin held a paw up. "No hating on my pugly magnificence. I'll wear you down, sweet cheeks. We're meant to be together. The Romeo and Juliet of the pug and poodle world." Colin waggled his eyebrows and pranced back into the kitchen.

Delilah stared, shocked, at the pug's exit. She recovered with a start and smiled with mock contriteness at Lila. "I'm sorry your meeting with the lovely reaper had to be cut short. Such a shame. Matthew's quite a delight. And that Zachary, such a sweetheart to help us out whenever we need it." Delilah winked at Lila and Xandie.

Melody took a step back. "I've suddenly lost my need for caffeine. My hairless eyebrows will catch you later." The bear shifter ducked out of the bakery at lightning speed.

Strolling around, the Devlin matriarch smiled winningly at any male patron she came across. "One does have to love a man in uniform or one that comes with a size-changing scythe." Delilah shivered and licked her lips. "Point Muse has become quite appealing for my family."

"*Why you...*" Lila launched herself around the edge of the counter, her hangover forgotten as she slammed to a halt when Xandie grabbed the back of her shirt.

"Take it easy, baker. She's deliberately trying to aggravate you."

"Lila? You okay?" Matthew cleared the last few steps from his upstairs apartment and stood confused.

"Matthew. How lovely to see you again." Delilah flounced up and latched onto one of his arms. "Such a strong boy. Have I said that before?" She squeezed his bicep. "You see that, Kali? The reaper's made of fine stock." She winked at the room.

"Let me at her." Lila strained at Xandie's grip. Who knew the Librarian had so much muscle.

Looking awkward, the reaper tried to unsuccessfully disentangle himself.

The customers in the bakery watched Delilah, whispering between themselves. The noise level in the room rose as the onlookers enjoyed the drama.

The kitchen door slammed open, hitting the wall with a crack of impending doom as Elspeth stalked out.

The bakery customers who'd been enjoying the show immediately ceased talking and dropped their heads down, pretending interest in their food.

"Fine stock has property of the Harrow family stamped all over him. Best you get your poisonous little claws off him."

Curling her lip, Delilah made a show of leaning against Grim's shoulder. "Or what?"

Elspeth swelled, her short turquoise wig seemed to wave with a crackle of static electricity as the lights flickered overhead.

"Excuse me, ladies, but I need to start work." Matthew quickly pried Delilah loose and retreated into the office at breakneck speed.

"Coward," Lila growled at her boyfriend.

Xandie released her cousin. "Are you good now?"

Sniffing, Lila jerked her head at their grandmother.

"I'll let the crazy lady deal with her nemesis.

That way I can deny any involvement if things go wrong, but still claim victory if Elspeth triumphs in the biddy-on-biddy action."

"Wise choice."

Both girls settled against the counter and waited for the fireworks to begin.

"Did I miss anything?" Hester, Lila's employee and the family Brownie, slid up next to them, munching on a chocolate slice. "Territorial squabbles always make me hungry."

Lila hushed Hester and focused on Elspeth. As much as she dreaded the fallout from Elspeth-caused mayhem, she couldn't help but want to see the overly flirtatious elderly lecher of the Devlin clan get her botoxed booty handed to her.

"Poodle got your tongue, Harrow? I said *or what?*" Delilah smirked as Kali crouched, hackles standing on end, growling.

"Now, hang on, sweet cheeks. You're cute and all that, and I can see pugly poodle puppies in our future, but no one growls at my Queen of mayhem. You go through me first." Colin shot past Elspeth to stand in front of her, protecting his wicked witch of Point Muse.

Shadows flickered around the edges of the room,

dimming the natural light of the bakery. A silent drone of anticipation covered all onlookers.

A slight vibration underfoot was the only indication of Elspeth's mood. She smiled slowly, her dentures sharp and prominent. "No *or what*. You do what I say, or I take you out of the picture. It's as simple as that."

Delilah clapped her hands, her heavily made-up face trying to smile. "I love a good threat first thing in the morning. Makes an old girl feel and look alive. But you must battle to keep yourself looking so young." The Devlin matriarch shuddered. "I'd never step out of the house if I looked as old as you."

Waving a finger, a shadow broke off from Elspeth and shot toward Delilah. It zoomed in on the dark witch like a heat-seeking shadow missile.

With a casual flick of her kitten-heeled shoes, Delilah kicked the shadow away. It careened through the air until it hit the opposite wall near the giant hearth. With an audible splat, it slid down, leaving a mucky gray stain on the wall.

As much as Lila wanted to see Delilah get her comeuppance, her much loved bakery would suffer. Time to put a stop to the elderly witch's grudge-filled shenanigans. Sighing, Lila stomped in between the duo and held her hands up. "You're both old enough to behave and having a grudge match in a public space where innocents can get hurt is a big no-no. Take it outside if you want to rumble. Just make sure you tell us when so we can sell tickets."

The two women froze for a moment, but Elspeth backed down with a mirth-filled cackle. Shadows receded and the lights in the room suddenly blazed, illuminating every line and wrinkle on Delilah's heavily made-up face.

"The youngster normally babbles garbage, but this time she's right. Public space is out. I'll extend an invitation for our next meeting in a more secluded space." Elspeth turned to Hester and pointed to an apple cupcake. "Feed an old witch, Hester?"

Delilah shuffled forward. "I suppose I'm a tad hungry now too. Maybe it *is* time for a snack."

Perusing her culinary options, Delilah pointed to the cake that Hester had dished up for Elspeth. "You know what? I love the look of that. I'll have one of those too."

Hester looked at the other witch like she was a bug on her no-nonsense sneakers. "It's an apple *Dutch Courage* cupcake and it's the last one."

"I am sure Elspeth won't mind sharing. I mean, we are old friends, after all." Delilah fluttered her eyelashes and grabbed the plate with the cupcake.

"Not so fast, Devlin. I have a hankering for an apple cupcake, and I ordered it first." Elspeth grabbed the other side of the plate and tugged it toward herself.

Delilah reacted and tugged back. The cupcake wobbled on the plate and tilted to one side.

"Elspeth," Lila warned. "I do not want to buy new china plates. Watch it."

"Fine..." Elspeth drew out the word and one finger at a time, released the plate.

Squeaking, Delilah grabbed the cupcake before it hit the ground.

"Careful there, sweetie. Hate for the last apple cupcake to end up on the floor."

"Thanks for your concern, Harrow. But I'm good." Delilah picked up the cupcake and let it hover in front of the mouth, savoring the scent of apple.

Lila's Harrow hackles rose as Elspeth's eyes glinted with glee. Elspeth-caused mayhem was afoot.

"Suit yourself." Elspeth crossed her arms as she waited for Delilah to taste the cupcake.

Making a big production of taking a mouthful. Delilah chewed the cupcake. "Not bad, nice tart flavor. Mixed with a sweet aftertaste. Light touch to the baking. Quite tolerable. Not as good as my girls, of course. But not bad overall." Delilah's words trailed off as she coughed, and then coughed a second time.

Not another choking death. Lila grimaced and squeezed her eyes closed. A growl sounded nearby, and Lila quickly opened her eyes. If a killer poodle attack was imminent, she needed to see the bite coming.

Delilah growled and pointed a trembling finger at Elspeth. She opened her mouth and a stream of gibberish poured out. "Tissue all youth, all of El Dorado."

"What was that you said, dear? I couldn't understand you." Elspeth held a hand up to her ear.

"El Dorado. El Dorado." Delilah stamped a foot and shook her fist at Elspeth.

Rocking back and forth with a deep belly laugh, Elspeth drew in a shuddering breath. "Never trust someone who compromises, Devlin. And always look a gift horse in the mouth."

Delilah mimed choking Elspeth, her eyes shooting metaphorical flames of retribution at the Harrow witch.

"Fluff a duck, El Dorado." Delilah gathered her killer poodle to her side and fled the bakery.

"You know that won't end well," Lila warned her grandmother.

"Eh." Elspeth shrugged. "She needs to learn to keep her overly manicured mitts to herself."

"We'll see if you feel the same way when she retaliates."

Elspeth rubbed her hands together. "Let the hex wars begin."

Hopefully Point Muse would still be standing when the smoke cleared.

SEVEN

"Time to harden up, Princess. This is war."

"It's dinner, Mother. And you fired the opening shot this morning. This is all your fault." Winifred bustled around the kitchen of Harrow House, putting together tacos for the family dinner.

"Which you then spoiled by dosing her with the antidote." Elspeth shook her long red braids. "I'm ashamed."

Winifred slammed a packet of cheese on the bench. "Don't you start with me, Elspeth Harrow. You're lucky I have antidotes for all your dirty tricks. I'm tired of cleaning up your messes."

Everyone in the room inhaled and stepped back. Even Harrow House shuddered as it waited for the explosion.

Lila rubbed a hand over a wall and crooned. Harrow House, a purple and black Victorian two-story, had always protected the Harrows. Generations of the family had lived, loved, and spelled within the confines of the house. To the point that Harrow House had become sentient and stubborn... *Very stubborn.* The house had a strong streak of quirky humor and wasn't above moving walls, stairs, and doors, to prank someone. Extremely protective, it always let them know when someone lurked outside. And it knew you never tangled with Elspeth Harrow if you wanted a long and mayhem-free life.

Elspeth considered her youngest daughter. "Why, Winifred. I do believe you've discovered your spine." She winked at her daughter. Everyone, including Harrow House, sighed in relief.

"I've always had a spine, but mostly, I prefer to stay in the background. Less migraines that way." Winifred pointed a taco at her mother. "But I'm tired of providing the cure for your mayhem, Mother. And now that Delilah's in town, I know what will happen."

Elspeth rested her head on one hand and a small smile twitched the corners of the mouth. "Do tell, brave daughter."

"Delilah will strike back, then you'll counter-strike, and it will disintegrate into a hex free-for-all. The body count will rise because the killer knows everyone's distracted by your hex war." Winifred glared at her mother. "Am I wrong?"

Amelia strolled in with her husband, Shade, by her side. "Is this the *stop hexing people because I'm tired of cleaning up your messes* argument?" She dropped into a seat at the dining table.

Lila nodded at her parents. "Same argument. But Elspeth hasn't wicked witched yet. Her restraint is surprising."

"Maybe her sanity is stabilizing in her old age." Amelia ignored the black look her mother shot her. She glanced around the room. "Where are your significant others, girls? Surprisingly light on testosterone in here."

"Elspeth told the guys a different time for dinner. She wants to talk Devlin strategy." Holly wandered into the room, eyes downcast as she flicked through a folder of loose papers.

Holly wasn't a big reader like Xandie, so why the sudden obsession with paperwork? "What are you reading there, death girl?"

Hugging the folder close to her chest, Holly blinked rapidly. "Work stuff. Nothing you need to read."

"Ah huh. Methinks the banshee doth protest too much."

Holly caved. "Fine. I'll tell you, but no one's reading the report. It's entrusted to me by my bosses."

"The freaky twins." Holly's bosses were descendants of Charon, the ferryman, who transported souls across the rivers Styx and Acheron. They were also necromancers who owned and ran the Elysian Fields Funeral Home. *And* they loved black velvet and raised Lila's heebie-jeebie hackles.

Holly glared at her cousin. "Don't call them that. They're good bosses and do what they can to help Point Muse and Chief Braun."

That explained the folder. Lila pointed at the paperwork. "I take it that's the autopsy results for Elaine Purdy?"

"Preliminary results. My bosses asked me to give it to Braun at dinner."

"Stop building drama. Give it to us straight." Elspeth tapped her fingers on the table. Blue sparks of electricity flared every time her neon green-painted nails hit the surface.

"Elaine was poisoned by a choking hex. Main ingredient was a heavy dose of Borage. Her throat closed over and blisters had formed at the back of her throat." Holly shuddered. "Nasty way to go, if you ask me."

She wasn't wrong. "Any results about my food?"

"The bulk of your stock came up clean, except for the tray of slices that Pastor Moss bought off you."

"See. Someone *is* out to get me and my granddaughter, and this is all happening after Delilah Devlin hit town."

"Technically, the hair poisoning happened before she turned up." Xandie strolled in, followed by Braun and Matthew Grim.

"Who knows when she arrived in town. She could've been hiding." Elspeth pointed to Braun. "Who let the fuzz in here?"

"Harrow house likes Zach and Matthew." Xandie gave her Aunt Winifred a hug. "Mom sends her apologies. She's been called out of town for a consult and won't be at dinner."

Xandie's mother, Miranda, sometimes consulted with the Paranormal Investigative Group or PIG for short.

"The house knows better." Elspeth glared at Braun. "And I suppose you're still on your poor innocent Devlin kick."

Zach rubbed his head. "I don't want to convict without evidence. If it's any consolation, we *are* looking into the Devlins' background as well as trying to ascertain any links between the hair loss incident and Ms. Purdy's poisoning."

"My food," Lila added morosely.

"Other than that." Braun paused for a moment and considered Lila. "We all know you aren't the killer, but I have to have evidence proving your innocence or implicating someone else. Everything has to be above board, considering my connection to the family."

Matthew sauntered over and leaned against Lila's chair. "We just need to find another viable suspect and show reasonable doubt in your case. But you need to give us time to do that."

Lila growled. "Meanwhile, my business suffers and someone else might be targeted by the killer. And you both refuse to consider the Devlins."

Elspeth clapped. "Well said, baker."

"The dessert bakery hasn't opened yet and the only connection they have to Point Muse is Elspeth."

"And Lila's my granddaughter, and the town baker. They want to sabotage her business. What other evidence do you need?"

"Elspeth, I promise you, we *are* looking at the Devlins. Currently, nothing in their background indicates murder. Unless you have access to other information?"

"Why... I..." Elspeth stuttered to a stop. A frown creasing her forehead. "Delilah's modus operandi is lovelorn suffering, and she may have driven some of her victims to suicide, but as far as I know, she's never outright killed anyone. But there's always a first time." Elspeth stubbornly jutted her jaw out.

Lila held up a hand. "I have no clue about a connection to the Devlins other than me, but I do know of a connection between Laura-Jean and Elaine Purdy."

The room waited for Lila to divulge the connection.

"Tell us." Holly stamped her foot. "I can't stand the suspense."

"It's obvious. They both belong to the Church of the Repentant Creature."

The room exploded into noise as everyone unloaded their opinions.

"I told you that church was bad news. That Pastor is way too good-looking. He stirs up the oldies. Anarchy is on its way." Elspeth nodded. "I'm always right. You should listen to me more."

Winifred shook her head. "That nice pastor has nothing to do with this."

"Just like those nice Devlins aren't involved?" Lila raised an eyebrow. "Someone's poisoning my customers."

Braun cleared his throat. "I'm assuming Holly's already filled you in on the preliminary test results. The bosses rang me and gave me a verbal update as well."

"Does that mean they don't trust Holly not to blab to the family?"

"Hey," Holly protested. "Don't hate on me. It's your customers getting poisoned after all."

"As I was saying," Braun overrode the cousins' squabbling. "Ms. Purdy was poisoned with a choking hex." He looked straight at Elspeth. "I need to check your hexed stock, Elspeth."

"Once again, a poor innocent Harrow woman is persecuted and unfairly blamed for murder."

"In his defense, we kind of have a reputation for discovering bodies and you *are* the wicked witch of Point Muse with a talent for hexing," Xandie pointed out fairly.

"I'll remember this, bear shifter." Elspeth stood but paused as Colin waddled into the kitchen.

"Hey, the whole gang's here. What's the news, witches?"

Elspeth pointed at Braun. "The fuzz thinks Lila

and I are murderers in cahoots and are using my hexes to carry out our nefarious agenda. He's raiding Harrow house right now."

Colin scratched his ear. "So, nothing new then."

"Your hexes, Elspeth?" Braun prodded the Harrow matriarch.

"This way to my den of iniquity then, copper." Elspeth flounced out the back door and led a procession of Braun, Grim, Lila, and Colin down to her potion shed. She flung the door to the shed wide open. "Have at it, shifter. But make sure you clean up after yourself. I keep a clean and tidy workplace. Everything in its place."

Braun stepped inside. "Is this the place you're talking about? Because it doesn't seem as tidy as you said it was. Frankly, your hexed shed looks like a tornado has rolled through."

"What?" Elspeth shrieked and shoved past Lila and Grim, who'd crowded in behind Braun. "This wasn't me. I've been robbed. Call the police. A crime's been committed." She spun and pointed a shaking finger at Braun. Electricity wreathed her hand and travelled along her arm. "I've been violated. I want the whole station working on this heinous crime."

"Robbery trumps murder?"

"Yes. When it's my territory defiled, it does." Elspeth stamped her foot. "Look at this mess, it will take weeks to settle everything and restock anything destroyed."

"Can you tell me if any of your stock is missing?" Lila poked her head around Grim and took in the devastation. Anything that had sat on Elspeth's shelves in organized and labelled potion bottles now decorated the floor. Cupboards and drawers lay emptied and upturned. A noxious green vapor hovered in one corner of the shed and a pungent, rotting fruit smell permeated the small space.

Grim stepped back, so Lila could have a better look at the destroyed shed.

"Not at first glance." Elspeth shoved a foot out and toed the pile of broken bottles. "Some of my premade hexes were in colorful bottles ready for shipping. They don't look like they're here."

"Goldilocks' mange," Braun swore. "This means someone may have access to more of your hexes?"

"Yep." Elspeth nodded.

"I need a list of your missing hexes as soon as you can." Braun stepped out, with Elspeth following at his heels.

Lila eased away from the shed and walked toward Matthew, who'd turned his back on the crime scene and was scanning the tree line of the national park that bordered Harrow House land.

"What's wrong?" Lila slipped an arm around her boyfriend's waist.

"Can you see movement out there? I thought I saw something."

"It's getting dark, maybe it's just shadows?"

"I don't think so." Grim pointed to a particularly thick shadow that had grown legs and arms. "Pretty sure that's a human-sized shadow."

Lila raised her voice. "Elspeth, looks like we have visitors."

"Eh?" Elspeth turned to face Lila. "No one's due for a visit except you hangers-on."

"I beg to differ." Lila pointed at the small group of men that had stepped out of the tree line and were marching toward Harrow House.

Braun nodded to Grim and the men stepped forward.

A faint noise drifted over from the uninvited group.

"Singing?" Lila strained to hear, following behind Braun and Grim.

A grey-haired, older man stepped forward. With his hand on his heart, he broke into song. His backup singers warbled along with him. "*When the moon hits your eye...*"

"*Hecate's tone-deaf ears. He's singing that old song. That's Amore.*"

Grim looked askance at Lila. "What old song?"

"Aunt Winifred always plays it when she's feeling soppy."

Lila slapped a hand over her mouth, stifling her giggles.

Braun raised his voice. "You need to move along. You're uninvited on private property."

One of the backup singers stopped singing. "You can't stop us declaring our love for Elspeth Harrow. She's our love goddess and must honor us with her favor."

"Has he met your grandmother?"

Lila exploded into gales of laughter at Matthew's comment. She bent over, gasping. Elspeth inspired something all right, but it wasn't normally love.

Lights on the porch of Harrow House snapped on, and the rest of the family crowded onto the porch.

The lovestruck singing trespassers raised their voices and belted out the love ballad.

"I've had just about enough of this." Elspeth appeared next to Lila and lifted a spelled hose. She clicked the trigger and the enchanted water hose spat water out in a thick stream that soaked the group of singers.

"This is Delilah Devlin. Has her nauseating touch of smaltz on it."

The men's singing stumbled to a stop as one after another copped a soaking from Elspeth's water hose.

"Vacate the premises and I won't arrest you for disturbing the peace. I'm sure Elspeth would appreciate you all leaving."

The group conversed together, and the same man who'd originally stepped forward spoke. "If Elspeth wants us to leave, we will. As long as she knows our love is eternal and we'll always be watching her.

Elspeth dropped the hose. "That love hex will dissolve by tomorrow. So, the stalking should then stop. That Devlin has a nasty streak, I'll give her that." Elspeth sniffed and disappeared back into her trashed hex shed.

Delilah wasn't the only one with a nasty streak. Elspeth did too... And the hex war had only just begun.

EIGHT

"It's D-day. Devlin dessert day. Ready battle stations. Gird your loins." Elspeth paced in front of Lila's bakery window. Every so often she'd stop and peer out at the crowd gathered out the front of the *Devilish Desserts Bakery*.

"Drama much?" Lila eyed her grandmother. Elspeth had turned up this morning, all dressed in black, with a matching black hoodie and long black ponytail wig. She looked more like the Grim Reaper than the actual reaper did.

"It's just an opening. Nothing to worry about." Aggie Braun, Zach Braun's mother, and another bear shifter, leaned back in a chair and ignored the creaks as the chair adjusted to her large frame.

"Just another opening?" Elspeth glared at her

friend. "Agatha Braun, hush your mouth." Elspeth paced, muttering under her breath about traitorous friends.

"It's never just an opening in Point Muse." Xandie stared glumly at her boyfriend directing traffic and sound outside the Devlins' storefront.

"Xandie, honey. You need to relax." The bear shifter patted the Librarian's hand. "Zachy bear loves you. He's just too nice for his own good." Aggie shrugged. "He gets that from his father. I'm meaner."

"He literally can't say no. They crook their fingers and he comes running with the reaper in tow." Xandie tapped her fingers on the table. "It irks me."

"You're a Harrow. Everything irks you."

"Right." Aggie pried herself out of Lila's chair. "I'm sick of your moaning. Let's go and see how the grand opening shakes out."

"Are you crazy?" Elspeth snapped. "Delilah Devlin will never let me forget it if she spots me at her party."

"Then make sure she doesn't see you, if you're that concerned about her opinion of you."

"I could care less what that woman thinks."

"Well then." Aggie smiled. "I guess we have a party to attend."

Lila waggled a finger at her grandmother. "Have fun. Do everything I'd do."

"You don't get out of it that easy." Xandie snagged an arm around her cousin and tugged her upright. "We need Harrows planted on the inside, gathering any proof we can of the Devlins' nefarious doings. Holly has to work and none of us can trust Elspeth. So, it's you and me."

"But... But what about the bakery?"

"The day I can't handle the bakery is the day I bury you." Hester stomped to the bakery door and flung it wide open. "Now get. I have my niece coming in a little while. I'm teaching her to bake. Clear out, Harrows."

"Fine, but I'm not going to enjoy a single second and will sneer at everything, got it?" Lila gave in and joined her family and Aggie on her bakery doorstep.

"You're a Harrow. We all know you whine. You put on your game faces, girls." Aggie fixed Elspeth with a no-nonsense stare. "That means best behavior, Elspeth. Don't give the biddies a chance to gossip."

"Yeah, yeah." Elspeth twitched her wig into place and adjusted the waistband of her jogging pants. "I'm ready and Colin and Nash are already over there keeping an eye on the Devlins."

"More like eating the Devlins' food." Lila took a

deep breath. She could do this without drama. It was just an opening. So what if the crowd outside their bakery was bigger than she got in a single day. Who cared? Time to suss out the competition and see how good the Devlins' food was. Lila led the group across the road.

Braun gawked at Xandie and Elspeth as they marched up. "Please tell me you aren't storming the bakery and taking no prisoners? I don't want to arrest my girlfriend or her grandmother for disturbing the peace."

"Hey." Lila poked Zach in the ribs. "Don't forget me."

"Or my girlfriend's cousin." He winced when he saw Aggie coming up behind the group of Harrows. "Or my mother."

Aggie patted her son on his cheek. "As if you could, Zachy bear. You have no chance taking us down. But fear not, we come in peace, don't we, girls?"

The Harrows muttered a muted yes.

Braun cleared his throat. "In that case, I hope you enjoy the opening. Grim's directing traffic inside, if you're interested, Lila."

Lila smiled sweetly. "Of course he is."

"Enough chittering. I have baked goods to tear

apart." Elspeth shoved past Braun and marched along the side of the waiting line before shoving her way inside. The others followed close behind.

The Devlins' dessert bakery hadn't changed much since Lila had liberated Nash from their blueberry pie clutches. Still glossy and gleaming with marble top tables and white subway tiles. The massive chandelier still hung from the roof, throwing shimmering patterns and shadows on creamy white walls. The late afternoon sun dappled through the large bay window at the front. The glossy black counter and a table at one end of the bakery were covered with plates of delicious desserts and glasses of champagne.

"Fine. I may have desert envy," Lila grumped.

"It isn't all about looks, it has to taste good as well," Xandie comforted her cousin.

"I'm mingling. You girls are on your own. Keep your eyes peeled for dodgy doings." Elspeth dragged Aggie over to an empty corner.

"Looks like most of the town's decided to visit."

"The Devlin sent out invites to everyone. Glad to see you guys turned up." Matthew glanced around and spotted Elspeth whispering in the corner.

Lila followed his eyes. "She promised Aggie she'd be on her best behavior."

"And you believed her?"

"I'm hoping the sheer numbers of collateral damage will limit her blast zone effectiveness." Lila glanced around the room. People had certainly turned up in droves. Pastor Ezekiel and his church cronies gathered in a clump. Chastity and Laura-Jean hovered nearby, and Horace Painter stood a few feet away, arms crossed, glaring at the entire room, and especially Ezekiel Moss.

"As long as Elspeth behaves herself, everything will be okay." Matthew brushed a kiss over Lila's cheek. "Try not to stress. Taste the food and keep an open mind. Colin and Nash seem impressed." The reaper pointed to a small, low set table set up with different doggy treats.

"That's not much of a compliment. Those two will eat anything." Lila held a hand up to forestall any comments. "I'll try to be nice, okay?"

Matthew agreed and, with one last glance, headed back to the front door.

Xandie waited for the reaper to walk out of hearing and rubbed her hands. "Right, what's our plan of attack?"

"I promised Matthew I'd play nice, so no mentioning attacks. Let's eat and just tear the food verbally apart." Heading to the buffet, Lila perused the offerings. Mini blueberry pies, black forest gateaux, and whoopie pies of all different flavors and colors filled one half of the table. The other half was decorated with mini rhubarb pies, tiny Boston cream pies, and different flavored cookies. Taking a plate, Lila piled it high with the delightful-looking desserts.

"My goodness, look at all the Harrows that turned up." Ruby beamed at Lila and Xandie

"Only three of us are here right now. Holly had to work, and my mom and aunt are busy," Lila offered as Xandie refused to speak.

"Holly's here. She arrived early." Rose joined her sister and pointed through the crowd at Holly. She'd piled her plate higher than Lila's and had chipmunk cheeks bulging with Devlin desserts.

As if sensing someone watching her, Holly lifted her head and her eyes widened as she spotted Lila and Xandie glaring at her. Holly immediately turned her back on her cousins and pretended she wasn't there, while still shoveling food in her mouth.

"She believes in storing food for the winter, I see." Delilah Devlin swept down the stairs from her apartment. "As long as that grandmother of yours is on her best behavior this afternoon." Delilah strolled closer to the counter where a banner proclaiming *grand opening* hung overhead. She raised her voice.

"Thank you so much to the wonderful residents of Point Muse who turned up to support my grand-daughters' bakery. Please eat up and be merry." The banner overhead suddenly sagged low on one side, causing the Devlin matriarch to let out a sharp squeak as it dropped toward her head.

Braun leapt forward and grabbed the banner before it collapsed on Delilah.

She laid a hand on his chest. "My hero, Zachary." The twins rushed to help.

"Happy to help, Delilah."

"I bet you are," Xandie muttered and left her plate on the table. "I think I've lost my appetite."

"You aren't the only one." Lila pointed out Agnes and her church cronies, glaring at Chastity and her friend.

"At least Laura-Jean has hair now," Xandie pointed out.

Laura-Jean must have visited Lila's Aunt Winifred. The previously hairless woman now sported an ultra-chic pixie cut. "It suits her. Hope-fully, she won't sue me now."

"Don't count on it," Xandie pointed out.

Delilah, now recovered from her banner shock, sauntered over to Chastity and Laura-Jean. Huddling close to the women, she whispered something to them. The trio shot sparking glances over at Agnes and her church minions.

Agnes's glare heated to radioactive as the Pastor joined his ex-wife.

Laura-Jean linked her arm through Ezekiel's and beamed up at him.

Holly wandered over and pretended to look surprised to see her cousins. "Gosh. I didn't think you'd come. I only just got here myself."

Lila rolled her eyes. "Give it up, chipmunk girl. We saw you stuffing your cheeks for winter."

"Hey," Holly protested. "I didn't think you'd come, and I wanted to taste their food. For research purposes."

"I want to hate the food, but it *is* delicious," Lila admitted. "The food's even put Laura-Jean in a good mood."

The Harrow cousins watched as Laura-Jean giggled and released the Pastor long enough to down the contents of a champagne glass someone had handed her. Then she snagged a plate laden with food from one of the church groupies and shoveled food at a lightning pace before shuffling back to the buffet for seconds.

"Whoa. If she doesn't stop inhaling, she'll burst at the seams." Lila couldn't believe how fast the normally curves-conscious woman put away the food. Even Chastity had noticed and stared open-mouthed at her friend.

Delilah, disgusted, turned her back on Laura-Jean.

Elspeth strolled over to her granddaughters, Colin and Nash with her. "Looks like someone can't get enough of the Devlin food."

Xandie peeked around Lila before ducking back behind her. "I can't watch. It's like a train wreck. I know something's coming, but I can't stop watching."

"Delilah's enjoying herself anyway." Lila pointed out the Devlin matriarch, who'd decided to make the rounds of the room, laughing and waving to the crowd of onlookers.

The older woman drew to a stop near Laura-Jean, with a slightly worried cast to her face.

"Nope, she's worried. I would be too." Colin sniffed the air. "Eau de desperation and gluttony. Smells like tuna."

Lila stared at the now rabid Laura-Jean, who'd abandoned all polite manners and had resorted to grabbing handfuls of the food from the buffet and shoving it into her mouth.

The reason hit Lila with an electric charge of a taser. "It's just like Elspeth's old coven member, who died at the diner. Laura-Jean's been hit with a gluttony hex." She turned to warn Grim, but it was too late.

Laura-Jean stopped shoveling food in and vomited on the floor. Her chest heaved and she had no chance to grab a breath between spasms. She dropped to her knees and slowly toppled over to lay still, eyes glazed and unblinking.

Delilah screeched and wrapped her arms about herself. "She's dead."

Ezekiel dropped to his knees next to Laura-Jean in search of a pulse. He shook his head and muttered a prayer over the woman's prone body.

"This is all your fault, Elspeth Harrow." Delilah pointed a shaking finger at her nemesis. "You've gone too far this time."

The crowd in the bakery turned as one and stared at Elspeth, horror written across their faces. The onlookers began to murmur behind their hands. Accusing glances centered solely on the Harrow family and Elspeth, in particular.

It looked like Point Muse was about to whip up a village mob and run Elspeth out of town... *Again...*

NINE

"At least no one can blame my food this time," Lila offered helpfully.

Xandie shot her cousin a withering glance. "Except some bright spark decided we should visit the grand opening. We were on site when the murder happened. Both you and Elspeth had motive and opportunity to poison Laura-Jean, and no one thinks the Devlins would poison one of their own customers at their own bakery opening. You and Elspeth are still the prime suspects."

"Maybe Delilah only meant to poison Laura-Jean? Like the hair incident, but it got out of hand?" Holly shuddered. "I still have that image in my head of her shoveling food in. It wasn't pretty."

Poor Laura-Jean had looked like a starved wild

woman as she attacked that buffet. A gluttony hex wasn't the way Lila would want to go. "Holly, do your bosses have any idea about Laura-Jean yet?"

"It's only been a few hours since Laura-Jean died. They haven't had a chance to perform an autopsy yet. Judging from her actions prior to death, they're pretty sure it was a gluttony hex."

"That doesn't help us at all," Xandie growled.

"It does kind of. There's a definite connection to the church again." Lila listed three points. "First, Laura-Jean and her pride in her hair. Second, Elaine and her lust over the Pastor. Then third, Laura-Jean again in her dessert gluttony."

"Oh." Holly's eyes widened as realization dawned. "You're right. The seven deadly sins."

"What?" Xandie looked confused.

Theo, Xandie's black cat, and an aging Greek guardian to the supernatural Great Library of Alexandria, strolled in. "You're a Librarian, how can you not know about the seven deadly sins?" Theo marched past Nash, Lila's hellhound. As he did, Horatio, Theo's pet imp, took a flying leap, his arms extended like a base jumper as he flung himself into the air. The imp landed on the hellhound's head, then slid sideways, until he hung off Nash's ear.

With a casual flick of his paw, Nash righted the imp, who settled down for a nap on the dog's back.

Ignoring the imp and hellhound's antics, Theo stalked around the Library, until he found a sunny area, and walked in a circle to find the warmest spot.

Xandie growled at her know-it-all cat. "You can't drop that word bomb and go to sleep. Elaborate, please."

Sighing, Theo stopped strutting around in a circle and sat. "You're in the Library. You could research. Isn't that what you're paid the big bucks for?"

"Technically, not paid. Now spill it."

"Fine. The seven deadly sins or the cardinal sins are a grouping of vices according to Christian religion. Pride, greed, wrath, envy, lust, gluttony, and sloth. I'm sure the Library would have scrolls, texts, or paintings on the subject. Now can I sleep? One does need one's beauty sleep."

"Nap away." Xandie turned Lila. "You think someone's poisoning and killing people according to the seven deadly sins?"

Lila nodded. "I think it's a definite possibility. At least, it's looking that way. If we're right, that means we have four more sins to go."

"You think it's church related." Holly pointed to

Lila, then swiveled her finger toward Xandie. "What does our great Librarian think?"

"I think Delilah and/or the Devlin twins are behind the killings."

"That logic or jealousy speaking?" Lila arched an eyebrow. "Hecate knows, I can't stand the Devlins, but they honestly looked shocked at their opening."

"The twins did. Not Delilah. I think she milked the situation for all it's worth. In my opinion, I think Delilah's the one we should be looking at." Xandie reached into her drawer, pulled out a folder, and slammed it down onto the surface of her desk. "That's why I did a background check on her family."

"Whoa." Lila held her hands up in a timeout. "Braun isn't going to be happy. That's his job."

"Then he should do it." Xandie glared at her cousin. "Do you want to hear the gory details or not?"

"Go ahead. Just be aware that wrath and envy are on the deadly sins list. No one wants a Harrow body on the body count."

"What she said." Holly pointed to Lila. "I kinda like the Devlins. They're a different kind of chaos to the Harrows. It's nice to have a change now and then."

"Now we've had that character reference, let's find out about Delilah." Xandie opened the folder and cleared her throat. "I'm paraphrasing, but the Devlins have quite a history. The family has always had a reputation for working on the dark side of witchcraft. Although some family members work grey magic. Most of their family gifts are centered around hexes, sex magic, love potions, et cetera. But they also have a pathological love of money."

Xandie flicked a couple of pages over and focused on the next lot of information. "Quite a few run-ins with the cops and a string of lawsuits. Bankrupting boyfriends is a favorite as is doing midnight flits after angry mobs threaten to run them out of town. There's a history of the family disappearing after a spate of unexplained deaths wherever they settle."

Lila interrupted her cousin. "They're Elspeth, but with sex magic and love potions?"

Ignoring Lila's interruption, Xandie continued. "Delilah herself moved around quite a lot. She's been named in too many divorces or court proceedings to count. Also, quite a few of her competitors have mysteriously gone out of business after she arrived in town. Delilah likes setting up potion stores and her last one was in Portland. Apparently, there's a charge of using substandard ingredients in her potions. She sold the last business a little while ago. Rumor is she injected a healthy cash donation into the twins' business."

On paper, old Delilah looked like a prime suspect, but if you read Elspeth's stats, so did she. Lila had a horrible fear they were missing a vital connection. Something that might cost someone else their life. "What about the twins?"

"Ruby and Rose Devlin have worked in Delilah's businesses for years. They seem to be closer to their grandmother than the rest of their family. For a while, one of Delilah's exes let them work in his bakery part time. Years later, their grandmother sells and stakes the twins here in Point Muse." Xandie looked up and grimaced. "From what my research tells me, they don't have much contact with the rest of the family now they've moved to Point Muse."

"They're the black sheep of the Devlin family?" They had more in common than Lila thought. Didn't mean she had to like or trust them. They still had a hefty dose of their family's love of flirting, or as Elspeth put it, sin.

"Whatever." Xandie shuffled the papers and slipped them back into the folder. "The point is the Devlins have a past and we shouldn't discount them.

The seven deadly sins idea is a good basis. But what's to say Delilah isn't framing the church or you for the murders? Anything to shift the spotlight from herself." Xandie pursed her lips. "No matter what my boyfriend says, I still think a Devlin is involved." She narrowed her eyes and dared her cousins to comment.

The Library's lights dimmed for a few seconds before the door slammed open and Elspeth rushed in. A panting Colin brought up the rear. "Hold the presses, witches. We got news."

"You know this is a Library, right? Not a newspaper."

"Enough sassing, Lila Harrow. The point is, I have news. Important news." Elspeth took a breath just as Colin ran between her legs and blurted the news out.

"Braun and Grim have taken the three Devlins to the station for questioning."

"Way to steal my limelight." Elspeth glared at a beaming pug.

"A pug's gotta do what he's gotta do to bring in the bread." He winked at Elspeth and strutted off to Nash.

"Ignore the pug." Xandie pounded her fist on the

desk, a big smile on her face. "It's about time my very smart boyfriend listened to me."

Lila cautioned her cousin. "Take a breath, victorious Librarian. He didn't arrest them. It's only an interview."

Xandie jumped up. "It doesn't matter. This is the first time Braun's taken his precious Devlins to the station. And I, for one, am not missing it. Girls, we have a police station to visit."

"Road trip," Colin sang as he danced to the door. "I call shotgun."

"Elspeth looks way too happy right now. I don't trust her," Lila whispered to Holly.

"She's got something planned. I can feel the potential for mayhem floating in the air." Holly shuddered. "Did I mention I'm over all the Harrow drama?"

Lila snorted. "Please, you're a Harrow. We're fed mayhem from birth. You'll never escape, just give in."

"That makes the Harrows sound like a cult."

"Shush. We need to listen." Xandie stepped up next to Elspeth as they watched through a two-way mirror as Braun interviewed Delilah.

Lila rolled her eyes and dragged Holly around the corner to the other mirror and watched Grim interview the twins.

"How come we can't hear anything?"

Aggie answered Lila's question by flipping a switch on the wall. "Remember what I said. Keep quiet and your boys will never know you're here."

Lila nodded her thanks but focused on the mirror as Matthew's voice filtered through.

"How well did you know Laura-Jean?" the Reaper questioned one of the twins.

Ruby bit her lip. "We didn't really know her. She popped in and introduced herself. She kept talking about the church and catering opportunities. We thought she oversaw the food and might give us the inside track on the jobs."

"Ha." Lila knew those Devlin girls had been scoping the competition.

The other twin piped up. "Honestly, other than that, we had nothing to do with her." Rose's eyes fluttered and she bit back a sob. "That poor woman. Who'd have the most to gain by sabotaging our business?"

Why that little... Lila thumped on the mirror, itching to get at the viper-tongued wench. Implying

Lila had sabotaged the food was a low blow, even for a Devlin.

Xandie bolted around the corner, eyes wild. She grabbed Lila. "We have a problem."

"Why do you always say that? It never ends well."

"It's all Elspeth. Nothing to do with me. You deal with her." Xandie shoved Lila at the cackling Elspeth.

Lila confronted her grandmother. "What did you do this time? Aggie warned us to be seen, not heard."

Elspeth pointed at the interview room. "It's not my fault the station has an infestation. Nothing to do with me."

Hecate's girded loins. What had her grandmother done? Lila peered in the mirror at Delilah and Braun. Everything seemed normal. But a tiny little shadow scuttled from the ceiling down to the floor, quickly scooting under the interview table.

Braun frowned and moved his chair back, trying to peer under the table.

Delilah watched Braun, a confused expression on her face, as she watched the policeman's antics.

Another shadow joined the first one under the table.

Delilah leapt up on a chair, screeching.

The two shadows formed into the shape of a metal stink bug.

Lila closed her eyes tightly before opening them and staring at her grandmother. "Tell me you didn't."

"What?" Elspeth spread her hands. "I have no clue what you're talking about."

A bloodcurdling scream erupted from Delilah and Braun's cursing of Harrow bloodlines came through clearly.

Delilah retched, hand to her mouth.

Breathing through his mouth, Braun dragged Delilah off her chair and up to the door of the interview room.

Quickly snagging Elspeth, Lila bolted away from the interview room. She deposited Elspeth next to Aggie's desk. Xandie and Holly joined them.

Delilah and Braun burst into the squad area, both sucking in heaving gasps of air.

"You." Delilah pointed at Elspeth. "This is all you. You're despicable."

"Eww." Elspeth wrinkled her nose. "Something stinks in here."

"Argh." Delilah launched herself at Elspeth, nails extended, looking for a target.

Caleb and Riley, Zach's younger brothers and deputies, pried the women apart.

Zach eyed the Harrows as Grim brought in the twins. "The Devlins are free to go, but don't leave town." Zach turned to Xandie and the rest of her family. "And you Harrows? Head home. The station will send out an invoice for the cleaning of our interview rooms." He glared at Elspeth. "Keep your nose clean, Harrow. I'm watching you."

"You'll never catch me, copper," Elspeth crowed and poked her tongue out at the departing Devlins.

Sometimes watching out for her grandmother felt like taking care of a crazed toddler.

One very evil toddler...

TEN

"Stalking is illegal."

"Only if you're caught, sweet cheeks." Colin scratched his side. "My Queen never gets caught. You need to be more like her."

"Only in my nightmares," Lila muttered and adjusted her position behind a particularly thick bush. She scratched her neck as an itch spread across her skin.

"Why are you hiding there?" Elspeth bit her lip, "I told you to hide behind that shrub." She pointed to a bush on the opposite side of the yard.

"Colin said this one." Lila rubbed again at the skin on her neck.

"Hey, I'm a pug. What do I know about directions?" Colin scratched his head. "Is anyone else itchy?"

Elspeth coughed and made a point of stepping away from the itching duo. "I said the other shrub for a reason. The bush you're huddled against is a staghorn sumac. Makes you itch."

"Seriously? This night couldn't get any worse." Lights highlighted the landscape around them as a car swung onto the road. She'd spoken too soon.

"Quick, over to the other bush." Elspeth scooted to the opposite side of the property and crouched in the shadows.

"Geronimo." Colin bounded past Lila and ducked behind the bush with Elspeth.

Lila scratched her neck and followed as quickly as she could. Her body was built for baking, not sprinting. She crouched next to Elspeth. "Do we need to spy on the twins? We only saw them a little while ago at the station. They can't have done anything nefarious in the meantime."

"We're gathering intelligence to use against the enemy."

"And why do I have to be here? You could have used Xandie or Holly on your spy mission."

Colin yawned. "They're following Delilah.

Xandie's worried my Queen would lose it if she had to spy on that evil witch. "

"Good point." Elspeth wasn't exactly known for her restraint.

"Down." Elspeth shot out her hands and shoved Lila and Colin's heads into the ground.

Lila spat out dirt. Dealing with Elspeth should come with hazard pay.

The lights from the car washed over the front lawn of the Devlins' rented house. Bertie Boxwood, an alchemist, had closed his shop and skipped town after a series of murders, including a poison peddler who'd shared shop space. Now the Devlin twins rented his tiny, two-bedroom home. Luckily for Lila and Elspeth, the house stood on the edge of town in a quiet deserted street. "How long do I have to eat dirt?" Lila whispered.

"Shush."

Huffing, Lila raised her head off the dirt a few inches and squinted. She could just make out a tiny white car that had pulled to a stop in the driveway. The twins climbed out of the car, both women glancing around before scuttling into the house. "Why are they in such a rush?"

"Why do you think?" Elspeth snorted. "Guilty conscience."

Colin scratched his head. "Can we go home yet? This itching makes me hungry."

"Suck it up, pug. We have a mission." Elspeth, crouching low, crab-walked down the side of Bertie's house. The wicked witch stuck to the shadows and away from the light shining from the house.

Following behind her grandmother, Lila froze as another light snapped on inside the house. Flattening herself against the building, she peered in through a tiny corner of the window that the curtain didn't fully cover.

The twins stood in a small bedroom. One of them paced, while the other stood on the spot wringing her hands. They looked worked up. Muffled tones breached the window as Lila strained to listen.

"No different..."

"Takes time..."

"Secrets..."

"Rid of..."

No matter what, Lila couldn't make out the full conversation. But what she heard was enough. Secrets and getting rid of someone certainly painted a definite picture. Lila inched back from the window to speak to Elspeth, but she and Colin had disappeared. "Seriously? It's like trying to herd a sugar-overdosed toddler." Scooting back to the front of the property, Lila dropped to the ground as she heard a rustling. Shadows thickened on the other side of the house, near the sumac shrub. Had Elspeth gone into wicked witch mode? Was her evil grandmother preparing to attack with malicious shadows?

"What are you watching?" Elspeth whispered from behind Lila.

Muffling her shriek, Lila growled at her grandmother. "Don't scare me like that. I thought you were on the other side of the house with those shadows."

"Why would you think that?"

"Because I heard a noise, saw the shadows and assumed it was you."

"You know what they say about assuming," Elspeth drawled.

"No? And who are *they*?"

"Forget it. You girls suck the life out of nefarious deeds."

"You still have me, sweetheart." Colin rubbed against Elspeth.

"And you're my sweet baby boy," Elspeth cooed to Colin.

"I think I threw up a little in my mouth." Seeing the wicked witch of Point Muse talking baby talk to an oversexed pug made her ill.

A loud bang on the other side of the driveway stopped all talk and the Devlins' porch light snapped on.

Elspeth yanked Lila to the side of the property.

Ruby Devlin marched out onto the porch, a wicked carving knife in hand. "Whoever is out there, you better scoot. My sister and I are armed with sharp weapons, and we've called the police. They'll be here any moment."

"Hekate's toenails," Elspeth cursed quietly and slowly backed up before turning and ducking next door.

"Elspeth! Don't you dare desert me," Lila hissed as quietly as she could.

Colin waddled past, keeping to Elspeth's tracks. "When my Queen retreats, best to follow her."

Lila rolled her eyes. Pearls of Harrow wisdom from a mouthy pug. She'd never live this down. Ducking under a low hanging branch, Lila sped up, trying to keep pace with her grandmother. Elspeth ducked and wove like a rabid octogenarian boxer.

They broke through the trees and bushes onto open grassland near a rickety shed.

Lila drew up next to her, breathing hard. "Why have we stopped? Isn't this someone's backyard?"

Elspeth caught her breath, before answering.

"We're all good. This is Edna's Witchshine shed. No way she'll call the fuzz if she hears us out here. She doesn't want to get busted again."

"Darn tooting. Whoever you are, get off my land or I'll send my boys after you." A woman's gravelly voice sounded loud in the dark backyard.

"I thought we were good," Lila hissed.

"I can't help it if she drinks her own product. It makes her crazy."

"I told you to get."

A crack sounded as something whizzed past Lila's ear. "Elspeth. She shot at us," Lila screeched.

"Run," Elspeth hollered, and gathered up Colin and bolted for the tree line.

"Thanks for the warning, Grandma," Lila shrieked and tried to follow the elderly Harrow sprinter but slipped on the wet ground, falling face first into a pile of dank smelling mud.

A spotlight blazed on and pinpointed a prone Lila.

"Why does this feel like déjà vu?" Braun's annoyed tones filled the air.

Lila sagged and let her head drop down into the mud with a squelching plop. Of all the Witchshine joints in town, he had to bust the one she lurked next to. Harrow bad luck strikes again.

Braun crouched down next to Lila, mud squelching over his boots. He tapped Lila on the back of the head. "You're not an ostrich, Lila, and this isn't sand."

Lifting her head, she spat out a mouthful of Witchshine-flavored mud. Edna's illegal still obviously had a leak. "This is all Elspeth's fault."

Zach checked his surroundings warily. "Is she lurking nearby about to hex me into releasing her favorite granddaughter from the police?"

"Xandie's her favorite, not me. She left me in the mud. She and Colin have probably hitchhiked back to Harrow House by now." Lila pushed herself up only for her hands to slip and send her face-first back into the mud, which flicked up in a splatter that covered Braun's pants legs.

Reaching down, Zach grabbed Lila under the arms and hoisted her to her feet. "Stalking is a crime, Harrow."

"I pointed that out to Elspeth, but she ignored me." Lila tipped her head to one side and tried to swipe the drying mud pack off her face, to no avail.

"I shot at Elspeth?" The tiny, grey-haired Edna shrieked and dropped the pellet gun. Unfortunately, the Witchshiner had already cocked the gun, so when it landed on the ground, it shot off a small pellet at Lila and Braun.

Cursing, the duo leapt out of the way, but both ended up back in the mud puddle together.

"I was dead asleep and saw nothing. I can't press any charges for trespassing. You hear me, Zachary Braun? I'm asleep." Edna slammed her back door and her lights switched off.

"That's one witness taken care of," Lila smirked, but her joke fell flat when she spotted Braun's scowling, mud-covered face. "Did I mention this is all Elspeth's fault yet?"

"Stop harassing the Devlins. All of them. I just dug Xandie and Holly out of the dumpster at the back of the Devlins bakery. They were searching for evidence. I spoke to the twins, and they don't want anyone arrested, but I'll give you the same warning I gave your cousins. Stay away from the Devlins."

"Tell that to Elspeth. But make sure you're wearing armor first." Lila slapped the puddle next to her and mud flew at Zach. "Oops. I'm sure Elspeth has a potion to remove that."

"That's it," Braun roared. He rose to all fours gingerly, then crawled out of the mud pit. "I'm done being nice in the face of mayhem. You reap what you sow, Harrow. Karma is coming your family's way."

Xandie's boyfriend had finally snapped. Mr. Nice Bear was gone and bearzilla stood in his place.

Elspeth better watch her back or the enraged bear shifter would drag the wicked witch to the lock-up, killer be damned.

ELEVEN

"Why am I being punished? I haven't offed anyone lately." Lila dumped an empty cake box in the trash.

"You and the Devlins need to learn to coexist in Point Muse. No better way than sharing a catering gig. Play nice."

Lila made a face. "When did you become creatively evil?"

"Hanging out with the Harrows." Braun crossed his arms and leaned against the counter. "You have to learn to roll with the chaos and adapt. Or you'll go insane every time Elspeth carries out her maniacal capers."

"Caper's a good word. Another is psychotic." Lila shrugged. "We're used to it. Still doesn't mean you should punish me."

"Let it go, Harrow. The man's doing his best. It's not his fault you Harrows are obsessed with mayhem." Hester, Lila's brownie and bakery employee, shuffled into the Point Muse Academy's kitchen.

"Elspeth. Not me," Lila pointed out. "The rest of us try to avoid the fallout."

Dropping a metal serving platter onto the kitchen bench with a loud clang, Hester scowled. "Who cares? How about we focus on getting our food out to the churches before they riot?"

"Point Muse Academy would love that." The Academy had offered up their hall to the town for community activities...as long as you paid for it. And the Church of the Repentant Creature had money to burn if the offered catering rates were any indication. "You're right, Hester. Let's get our food out there."

"That's my cue to leave. But I'll be lurking, Lila. No funny business."

"Don't bother watching me, you'll be too busy fending off the old biddies looking for dance partners. Xandie will be green-eyed with jealousy."

"This bear don't dance."

The kitchen door swung open, nearly knocking the police chief out. Ruby Devlin rushed through. She paused when she noticed Braun standing close to the door. "Zach. I didn't see you there. I hope I didn't hit you with the door. It's such a madhouse out there." She swiped away a lock of hair that had slipped from her messy bun.

"All good, Ruby." He smiled down at the flustered woman. "I take it the dancing has started?"

"I didn't realize Point Muse had so many people interested in a church dance. The dance floor is packed and people are already asking when the food's coming out."

"Point Muse loves a party even with a crazed killer running around."

"Point Muse law enforcement will make sure nothing happens at the dance."

Ruby fluttered her eyelashes. "Of course not. We know you'll keep us safe, Zachy."

Lila coughed into a hand. "Loser."

"Remember what I said, Lila." Braun nodded to Ruby and stalked back out to the dance.

Bouncing forward, Ruby grabbed Lila's hands and gripped them tightly. "I know this isn't ideal, Lila, but I'm glad we're both here together."

"Safety in numbers, I guess." According to Elspeth, the Devlins were the devil's grandchildren. If she were honest, they were starting to grow on her.

"Let the baker go, Ruby. You'll make things

weird. Plus, she needs to get her food out." Rose Devlin marched into the kitchen.

Looking embarrassed, Ruby dropped Lila's hands. "Sorry. I get carried away sometimes. It's a family thing."

"Speaking of family, I should warn you…"

Lila waved Hester past as the brownie stomped up, laden with a platter of food. Lila held the door open so she could shuffle through. Dancers crowded the edges of the hall as the dance floor overflowed. Lila spotted a familiar bewigged family member dressed in a hot pink jogging suit. Lila let the door slam shut. "Let me guess. My grandmother decided to turn up after all."

Rose looked surprised. "Actually, I was about to tell you, Delilah turned up too. I wanted to give you a heads up."

"We need more than a heads up if those two are in the same room." Lila grabbed another platter piled high with tiny finger sandwiches. "Thanks for the warning," she added grudgingly. Stepping out into the hall, Lila paused as the atmosphere of the church dance hit her. Typical Point Muse. Even with a killer on the loose, no one got between the town and a good party.

"I'm surprised so many people turned out."

Xandie pushed through the crowd to Lila's side. She snatched a tiny chicken sandwich and munched appreciatively. "Oh, that's yummy."

"Glad you appreciate my efforts. Now keep your mitts off my food." Lila shifted the platter away from her cousin and plowed through the crowded room. She sighed in relief when she'd delivered the sandwiches to the food-laden table without incident.

"How is it working out with our mortal enemies?" Xandie cast a hungry gaze at the food offerings.

"Not bad, actually. Say what you will about the family, they know their food."

Xandie scowled. "I see you're changing your tune. Have Grim and Braun gotten to you?"

Lila rubbed her forehead. The noise of the live band and people having a good old time had produced one epic headache, and it wasn't even Elspeth-caused... *Yet.*

"No one's gotten to me. I just think the twins' food is good. That's all."

"As long as you aren't wavering over to their side. Harrows have to stick together."

"Aren't you a Meyers?"

"Close enough. Even a drop of Harrow blood counts."

Lila sighed. "Look, I just want to get through tonight body free. I can't handle any more chaos right now."

Xandie considered her cousin for a moment. "Why don't you go outside and get some fresh air. Hester and I can handle bringing the rest of the food out and Holly should be here soon too."

"Can you play nice?"

"If I have to. Go get your fresh air."

Lila nodded her thanks and weaved her way to the exit. She shuddered when she spotted a pink-clad, rainbow wig-wearing Elspeth, boot scooting in the middle of the dance floor. Coincidentally, Delilah stood on the opposite side of the dance floor, holding court in a short lavender floaty dress with knee-high, white, go-go boots. "Fresh air sounds good right about now." Pushing the doors open, she stepped into the cool night air and took a few deep bracing breaths.

Another couple stumbled out, shoving Lila to the side as they giggled and groped each other.

"Man, the oldies sure know how to party." Lila headed around the side of the building away from the amorous couple. She leaned against the hall with a sigh of relief.

"I need money."

"Why speak to me? Your ex-husband has plenty and can't seem to say no to you."

Lila drew back into the shadows and hugged the building tight. She couldn't see the speakers but one of them was definitely Chastity Moss. Her high-pitched tones were easily identifiable. As for the other woman, Lila had no clue, but she had to be connected to the church since Chastity knew her.

"Ezekiel put his foot down and his family have locked down their money. I can't access it."

"Why come to me?"

"Because, Janice, you're the secretary of the church. You handle all their money."

"And?" the other woman scoffed. "Just because I handle the church finances doesn't mean I'll give you money. Haven't you heard that's illegal?"

"When has illegal worried you? I've been doing some digging. Dorothy from that low-grade beauty parlor happily divulged all about those beauty treatments you've been having lately."

"That's not against the law."

"Beauty treatments aren't, but embezzling funds from the church to fund those treatments, is. What's a few more dollars for little old me?"

"Or?"

"Or my lovely judgmental ex-husband might

find out what you've been doing with the church books."

"You wouldn't dare."

"Oh, I would. I want out of this town and anything to do with this church. Ezekiel's groupies are dropping like flies, and I don't intend to be the next victim. You need to pay up or confess to Ezekiel how you funded your beauty treatments."

"You wouldn't dare, Chastity. I'll call your bluff. I'll tell him you blackmailed me."

"Don't threaten me. You have more to lose than I do. Give me the money or you'll regret it."

"There's plenty of secrets in this church. I know most of them. Don't threaten me or I'll spill everyone's secrets, and no one will even look at my money issues."

"Why, you little…"

Janice yawned. "You're wasting my time. I'm going to grab something to eat and then head home for an early night. Enjoy being penniless, Chastity. It's a new look for you."

Lila bit back laughter as Chastity screeched and stomped off, her footsteps loud enough to wake the dead. She made a mental point to speak to Dorothy from *Hair Today, Gone Tomorrow*, the local hair salon, beauty parlor, and gossip central. The hairdresser might have more details on the embezzling Janice. The church was looking more and more suspect.

"That Chastity's a piece of work, isn't she?" Agnes joined Lila in her shadowy hiding place.

"She's definitely something. Threats and black-mail aren't something you normally witness at a church dance."

"You haven't been to enough church activities then." Agnes paused for a moment. "I'd like to apologize to you."

"What about?"

"The catering issue. You having to share the catering and the payment with those Devlins."

Lila shrugged. "Braun's forcing me to cooperate with the Devlins. I think he's hoping we'll end up friends."

"The Police Chief had a meeting with Pastor Moss. This was both their idea. Ezekiel prefers everyone to get along. Can't stand discord."

Who could... Except maybe Elspeth? "Pastor Moss seems popular."

"Sometimes too popular," Agnes muttered.

"What do you mean?"

"Poor Ezekiel had to leave his last position. He was right in the middle of his divorce and every single female parishioner wanted to comfort him. It came to blows. And then there was the issue of Chastity."

Gossip. A sleuther's best research tool. "What kind of issues?"

"Chastity has a temper. A few of those parishioners suffered accidents. Not fatal, of course," Agnes rushed to add. "But they were questionable, and Chastity was seen lurking in the vicinity at the time. Never charged, but the rumor was she'd engineered the accidents to squeeze Ezekiel out of more money."

"What a peach." And totally in character for the Chastity she'd seen in Point Muse.

"Quite." Agnes straightened. "Excuse me, I need to make sure everything's running smoothly inside." She nodded to Lila and disappeared back into the hall.

Lila girded her baker's loins. "Guess I better see what damage Delilah and Elspeth have wrought." Pushing the door open, she stepped in and came to a stop, pleasantly surprised.

The mortal enemies still stood in separate corners holding court. No hexes had been thrown and everything seemed relatively quiet. Lila glanced around the room, Hester and Xandie had brought all the food out, and people already lined up at the buffet table.

"No one's dropped dead yet. But I'm volunteering Braun for the role of the next victim." Xandie pointed to her boyfriend as he boogied past them with Ruby in a snaking conga line.

"I thought bears didn't dance."

"Apparently, when Ruby Devlin asks, he does." Xandie glowered at the shifter.

"Never mind." Lila slapped Xandie on the back. "As long as everyone's eating and no one drops dead, I count this night as a win."

"About that."

"What?"

Xandie bit her lip. "Now, don't freak out."

"Just tell me." Lila gritted her teeth. She wanted this night to be mayhem free, but it didn't look like she'd get her wish.

"Nobody's eating your food. They're only eating the Devlins."

Lila sagged. In the scheme of things, she'd expected another body. People not eating her food wasn't the worst-case scenario she'd imagined.

"Earth to Lila? Aren't you worried?"

"No one's dead. That's all I'm worried about. As

long as I get paid, people can throw the food for all I care."

"You're a playboy, Moss. Someone needs to sort you out." Horace Painter's loud, belligerent voice suddenly carried over the noise of the crowd.

"I take it back. I don't want a food fight or any fight at all."

"Let's do a drive-by eavesdrop."

"Speaking of eavesdropping, I need to tell you what I heard outside."

"Hold that thought." Xandie positioned them just behind the warring duo.

"Horace, you need to lower your voice. You know this is an alcohol-free zone tonight," Ezekiel cautioned the tipsy man.

"I don't care." Horace slugged back a shot from his hip flask. "I'm sick of your pious attitude. You lead all the ladies on while still making googly eyes at that waste of space, Chastity." Horace shot out a hand and shoved the Pastor.

"Step back, Painter. This is my last warning." Ezekiel glared at the elderly man. Anger transformed his normally calm face. Red flushed his pale cheeks and his eyes glittered.

First time Lila had seen another emotion other than calm acceptance on the man's face. The good old Pastor had a temper and Horace had riled him up.

"Gentlemen. A dance is not an appropriate time for this conversation. I suggest you go home and sober up, Horace," Agnes interrupted.

"You're nothing but his mouthpiece, Agnes." Horace wavered on his feet. "I'll be seeing you later, Ezekiel." He stumbled away through the crowd.

"Point Muse definitely lives up to its reputation." Rose strolled up with Grim in tow.

Matthew snagged Lila and buzzed her cheek with a quick kiss. "What's all the shouting about?"

"A drunken Horace Painter accusing the Pastor of being a playboy."

"And he isn't the only one." Xandie glared at Grim. "Seems Braun found his dancing feet."

"Sorry." Rose flashed Xandie a weak smile. "My sister can be persuasive. We're waiting for our date to turn up."

"Date?"

Rose beamed. "That lovely reporter, Percy. He agreed to partner us both. He's so sweet."

Sweet wasn't something Lila normally associated with the news-obsessed reporter. "I haven't seen him yet. Maybe he got wind of some other drama and is out scouting another story?"

"He'll be here. I'm just glad the church secretary paid us upfront. I'm not sure how this night will end." Rose looked around. "I think half the people in here are hiding hip flasks."

She wasn't wrong. "Hang on... You've already been paid?"

"She paid us as soon as we showed up tonight. Didn't she speak to you?"

"Nope." Lila forced a smile. "I think I'll find Janice and have a word. Excuse me." Ignoring her friends, Lila hurried off. Devlin was right, considering how a night of festivities in Point Muse normally ended. She needed to get paid, ASAP, before the next body dropped. Scanning the room, Lila spied the church secretary, sitting down in a corner near the coat rack. As she neared, Lila noticed the woman leaning against the wall, with her eyes closed. How could the secretary sleep with all the noise around her? Lila leaned over and shook the woman gently. "Janice? I need to speak to you about payment."

The woman failed to stir. Lila shook a little harder and raised her voice. "Janice? You need to wake up." The woman refused to twitch. Lila shot out a hand and fumbled at the woman's neck, trying to find a pulse.

"Everything okay?" Braun stood behind Lila, his Devlin arm candy absent.

Elspeth sauntered up. "That Janice can nap anywhere."

"I think it's a little more serious than that." Lila stepped back. "You need to call the healers; her pulse is way too slow. I don't think she's sleeping willingly."

Grabbing his phone, Braun spoke urgently into it.

Dragging Lila to the side, Elspeth whispered, "Narcolepsy hex."

"Excuse me?"

"That's what she's been dosed with. Narcolepsy or sleepy time hex. Your Aunt Winifred calls it a sloth hex. It's one of the potions that disappeared from my shed in the break-in."

Sloth, another deadly sin. Hopefully, it wouldn't end up fatal for poor Janice.

And Lila still hadn't been paid...

TWELVE

"Janice is in a coma. The healers flushed the hex out of her system, but she still hasn't woken up yet."

"I can't believe I missed all the drama."

"You ditched us to work late. It's your own fault." Holly had walked up minutes after the healers had taken Janice to the hospital. Braun had shut down the dance and taken all the food and drink for testing... *Again.* Lila sighed and shoved another *Decadent Death by Chocolate* brownie into her mouth. She let the rich chocolate flavor dissolve the bitter aftertaste from another failed function.

"Hey. Not my fault. My bosses needed me to unpack their new load of artifacts."

"You need to learn to say no, dear. *No.* It's not hard. Elspeth says it all the time." Dorothy Johnson, octogenarian hairdresser and co-owner of *Hair Today, Gone Tomorrow* hair and beauty parlor, pursed her lips. "Lila, sweetie. What have you been doing to your luscious curly locks? It's limp. No woman wants limp."

Lila rolled her eyes and refused to look at her sniggering cousin who sat next to her. Dorothy, and her sister-in-law, Olive, were Point Muse institutions. Gossip and hairdressing were a perfect mesh, especially for a sleuth looking for clues.

Olive yanked Holly's hair and tutted. "Don't you laugh, dear. Eau du death isn't attractive on a single female. Honestly, I thought Elspeth would've dealt with your desperate and dateless situation."

Holly snagged a chocolate brownie. "She gave up on us years ago. Lila and Xandie found their own boyfriends, so she thinks if she ignores me, I'll do the same," Holly smirked.

"Good luck with that. Not much call for a love of death here in Point Muse." Olive whipped out a pair of old fashion shears. "How about a trim?"

Holly choked on a mouthful of brownie. "I'm just here to gossip. Lila's the one visiting her boyfriend's parents.

"Whoa. Big step, Lila. You need an amazing

haircut for that." Dorothy clapped her hands. "Emergency care protocol. And...break."

Olive scooted to a painted white cupboard as quickly as her towering lavender beehive hairdo would allow. Opening the cupboard, she drew out a block of chocolate and from a small fridge next to the cupboard, drew out a chilled bottle of champagne.

"Kinda early in the day to drink, don't you think?" That stash of chocolate indicated serious sugar issues. Not to mention the champagne. Lila wondered just what happened in the hairdressing salon after hours.

"If you're visiting parents, you need emotional bolstering and a good conditioner. Our immersive beauty experience can provide that." Dorothy popped the cork and handed Lila a glass of bubbly and Olive shoved the block of chocolate in Lila's face.

Giving in, Lila accepted both. "We need to ask you a few things about Janice from the church."

"We'll talk after your hair's hydrated." Dorothy grabbed the champagne and handed it off to Olive and directed Lila to the basin. "Now, sit back and enjoy. We'll discuss murder while we trim."

Dorothy's fingers worked their magic on her head and Lila sagged into her chair. Murder, smurder. Hairdressers were where it was at. Humming in contentment, Lila closed her eyes, letting the drama from the last week drift away.

Dorothy slapped a towel around Lila's head and expertly wrapped her hair. "Right. Back into the chair, Harrow. I have just enough time to work a miracle."

Following dutifully, Lila settled back into her seat next to a bulging-cheeked Holly. "Again? Didn't you store enough for winter at the Devlins' grand opening?"

Holly mumbled around her mouthful. "I wanted to get into the chocolate before you did. We all know what you're like when it comes to cocoa and sugar. You might take my hand off."

Yanking the block of chocolate back, Lila grumbled as she assessed the damage. "Half? How could you fit half a block of chocolate in your mouth?"

Eventually swallowing her gigantic-sized mouthful, Holly grinned. "Talent I'm proud of."

"That's why you're single, darling." Dorothy expertly snipped away. "Now, Lila, you wanted information on poor Janice?"

"If you have any."

Olive snorted. "We have some. She was in hock to us for ten. All those beauty treatments add up."

"Ten dollars?"

Dorothy cackled and patted Holly on the cheek. "Such an innocent. Ten thousand dollars. She's been coming here three times a week since that cute Pastor came to town."

"Ten thousand?" Lila nearly spat the chocolate out before hurriedly swallowing. "She had that type of cash?"

"Nope. That's the problem. We were about to cut her off when she paid her tab."

"When did she get the money to pay her tab?"

Olive waggled her painted eyebrows. "She never came out and told us. But she mentioned robbing Peter to pay Paul. We kind of assumed she borrowed cash from the church books."

"Why on earth would the woman want to embezzle funds from her workplace to pay for glop on her face?"

"And that's why you're single, dear. That glop can create amazing results." Dorothy frowned at Holly and moved the champagne away from her.

"Janice stole money so she could look pretty for Ezekiel, who only has eyes for his trashy ex-wife?"

Olive nodded. "Pretty much. And let me tell you, that ex-wife is not a natural blonde."

"Plenty of women of all ages are atwitter over

that pretty Pastor. I prefer my men a bit more cave-man." Dorothy shivered. "Some of those church biddies are scary. He'll have a riot on his hands if he isn't careful."

"Nearly happened last night. A fight, not a riot." Lila had a feeling that Ezekiel and the church were at the center of all the current drama. "Horace Painter hit his hip flask heavily last night and accused the Pastor of being a playboy."

Dorothy sighed. "That man. I told him to lay off the Witchshine, but he has a special deal with Edna. He'll end up destroying every brain cell he has with that gut rot."

"Is there any truth to his words?" Holly leaned forward, interested.

"I call it BEM. Before Ezekiel Moss. Horace likes to play the field. Since the pretty pastor turned up, the playing field is dry. He is bitter."

"Envious and angry," Olive corrected her sister-in-law.

"Would you say wrathful?" Two more deadly sins for a killer to strike off their list.

"Probably both, but I think the envy edges the wrath out. Poor man." Olive handed the blow-dryer over to Dorothy.

"Know anything about Delilah Devlin?"

"Elspeth's nemesis? She wouldn't dare show her over-waxed eyebrows in here. We're solidly behind Elspeth."

"Safest place to be," agreed Olive.

"It was worth a try." Lila shrugged.

"Well…I did see her arguing with someone the other day. Couldn't see who was with her. But there was lots of finger-pointing, maybe a shove or two."

"Could you hear what they were talking about?"

"Something about following someone. Make her pay. That type of drivel. Delilah laughed and said she was just here to settle an old debt."

"Ha," Holly crowed. "Delilah's here to take Elspeth down. Settle an old debt. Now we have proof."

"It is all hearsay. Inadmissible in court." Dorothy hefted the blow-dryer but paused as the women stared at her. "What? I've gotten in enough tangles with Elspeth and the law to know a few things. Now everyone zip it. I'm creating here." Dorothy switched the blow-dryer on and went to work.

"Good hair, just don't care." Lila fluffed her bouncy curls as she strolled down Main Street.

"At least you aren't limp anymore," Holly snickered.

"You don't understand the pressure on my hair. Baking, girlfriend stuff, and now sleuthing. It takes it out of me. Especially my hair."

Holly rolled her eyes. "I'm happy to stay single and away from the mayhem. That way there is no meeting the parents stress you're going through currently."

Lila nibbled her lip. "Do you think they'll like me?"

"You're a Harrow. You probably will find somebody murdered and distract everyone."

"But will they like me?"

Holly sighed and stopped in the middle of the sidewalk. She grabbed Lila by the arms and gave her a little shake. "You're a Harrow with a radioactive warhead for a grandmother. You trump them. In the end, the only thing that matters is how Grim feels about you. Now stop it. You're freaking me out."

Lila took a deep breath. "I'll never say this again, but you're right. If they don't like me, I'll sic Elspeth onto them. How bad could it be?" She blew out a breath. "I feel so much better and I'm looking *fine,*" she sang the last sentence and wiggled on the spot in a weird twerking motion.

Holly covered her eyes. "Why torture me? You know I hate your victory dance. It's visually frightening."

"Pay for therapy. Because the dance is here to stay." Lila grabbed Holly and spun her around, nearly taking out a hunched-over Horace Painter.

"Watch where you're going, Harrows." The bleary-eyed man took a step to the side to avoid the women.

"Sorry, Mr. Painter." Lila shoved Holly to the side and smiled sweetly at the man. Nothing like interviewing a suspect when a girl looked her best.

"Just watch yourself."

Lila took a step in front of the hungover man. "I wanted to check on you. See if you're okay after last night."

Horace frowned at the perky Harrow. "Why shouldn't I be?"

Taking a page out of the Devlins' playbook, Lila fluttered eyelashes at the elderly man. "Because of poor Janice and the incident at the dance."

"Let me guess, she made a play for that playboy and his ex-wife shut her down?" Horace sneered.

Could he not know? "Janice was poisoned with a sloth hex last night. She's in a coma in the hospital."

Horace stared open-mouthed at Lila, before

grunting, "I always said that man's no good. No one listens. Now Point Muse's got another body. Typical."

"I take it you didn't see anything last night?"

"You can't blame me." Horace shoved his face close to Lila's. "I left early, remember? Nothing to do with me. You're the one with the poisonous food reputation."

Gagging on the man's noxious fumes of stale Witchshine and pungent onions, Lila waved a hand in front of her face. "Doesn't mean you didn't poison her before you left."

Drawing back, the elderly man let out a rusty chuckle. "True, but if I did, my target wouldn't have been mouthy Janice."

"Ezekiel." Lila filled in the gaps.

"Ding ding. The baker won a prize," Horace sneered at Lila. "Like all the other women in the church, Janice had a crush on the pretty boy and look where that got her." Horace shoved past Lila and yelled over his shoulder as he ambled off, "Better watch out. Everyone that makes googly eyes at the Pastor has dropped dead."

"I guess we can strike Horace off our suspect list. He had no idea about Janice's poisoning."

Lila stared at the man's retreating back. "Or his

acting is top notch and Horace hates Ezekiel and thinks all the murders are connected to the church."

"What do you think?"

"I think the body count will rise if we don't find the killer. Whoever it is." Plus, she had parents to impress and a reaper to charm with her well-coiffed locks...

Piece of cake for a witchy baker.

THIRTEEN

"Your parents own the building?" Lila stared up at the red brick and tinted glass frontage of the historic warehouse.

"Reaper Headquarters own the building. My family just has a floor in it. Other reaper families maintain offices here as well." Matthew ruffled Lila's hair. "Have I told you I like the curls? They're bouncy."

"Good hair, just don't care," Lila replied mechanically. Matthew's family actually worked in a historic, nineteenth century, restored warehouse in the Old Port District of Portland, Maine? Beautiful cobblestones, brick buildings, and a fishing pier jostled for attention with boutiques, gourmet cafés, retro restaurants, and happening bars. A lifetime away from sleepy–except for the odd murder–Point Muse.

"Seriously, it'll be fine. They're going to love you." Matthew tugged Lila into the building and up to the security desk. "Hey, Frank. How are the kids?"

An older man looked up and smiled at the couple. "Lolly delivered seven. We're trying to find homes for them all. And Lewis is mourning his lost virility since we sent him in for the snip."

"You have a daughter who delivered seven kids? She deserves a medal." No way would Lila pop out seven kids at once. *Talk about a fertility nightmare.*

Frank snorted. "Lolly and Lewis are Labrador Retrievers. They're our fur babies, Ms. Harrow."

"Phew. For a moment there you had me worried."

Matthew chuckled and handed over a pass. "Here you go, Frank. Can we sign Lila in?"

The security guard pushed the pass back to the reaper. "No need, Matthew. Your parents sorted all the paperwork out last week."

"How did his parents know we'd visit today when we only just decided to come?"

"That hoot of a grandmother of yours sent word." Frank shrugged. "Elspeth Harrow's famous. She knows everything. Now scoot on up, everyone's waiting on you."

"Yeah. Great." Lila forced her frozen body to follow Matthew as he ushered her into the elevator.

"Hold the doors." A man shoved a meaty hand through the gap between the elevator doors and pushed his way in. "Well, well. Look who we have slumming with us."

"Harrison." Matthew's voice remained calm, but his grip on Lila's hand tightened.

Since Frank, the security guard, had let this meatball through, he was obviously a reaper. One who Matthew didn't have a high opinion of by the lack of expression on her normally laid-back boyfriend's face. Lila studied the other man's thick neck and beady eyes. For that matter, she wasn't impressed either.

"Taking the little woman to meet the in-laws, Mattie?" The man slapped Matthew on his back and winked at Lila. "We all thought little Mattie too sensitive to ever find a girlie to put up with him." The elevator beeped and the doors opened on the man's level. He held the doors and eyed Lila up and down appreciatively. "What do you do? Dancing?"

Lila bit back her projectile vomit and peeled the man's fingers off the elevator door, one by one. "I babysit the wicked witch and find dead bodies in my downtime. Bye bye." Lila waggled her fingers in a wave and smirked victoriously as the doors closed in the reaper's shocked face.

Matthew burst out laughing. "My brothers will love that you put Harrison in his place."

"I take it you don't like the guy?"

"The Harrisons think reaping souls is a competition. The whole family is the same. No one can stand them."

The elevator dinged as it settled, and the doors opened onto a brightly lit hallway with a solid metal door at one end.

Lila swallowed the lump that had magically appeared in her throat. "I guess we're here."

Matthew brushed a kiss over Lila's white clenched knuckles. "I swear, it'll be fine."

"Let's get this over and done with." Lila took a deep breath.

The door swung open and Ed, Matthew's father, glared at them from the doorway. "Hurry up. Izzy wouldn't let us eat any of the Kung Pao chicken until you'd arrive and we're all hungry."

Lila followed Matthew as he headed in. "Your mother cooked us lunch? Should we have bought something? I can't visit without a gift or dessert if she cooked for us. It's against the girlfriend visiting the boyfriend's parents for the first time rule."

A large, dark-haired man with a bright red beard burst out laughing. "Mom cook? We'd never survive that."

Ed nodded. "Sadly, I agree with Lucas. I love my Izzy dearly, but cooking isn't one of her talents."

"But ordering from a local Chinese restaurant is." A tiny woman with flaming red hair, green eyes, and a slim build, bustled over to Lila. Ignoring her still-laughing son, she gathered Lila into a tight hug. "I'm so glad you're here. Elspeth told me you like Chinese. In honor of your arrival, we have a Chinese banquet prepared."

"Thanks. Nice to meet you, Mrs. Grim," she squeaked out.

"It's Izzy." Matthew's mother released Lila and frowned at her youngest son. "Next time, bring her for a weekend instead of a day trip. I want to get to know my soon-to-be, daughter-in-law."

"What?" Lila's shriek and Matthew's bellow combined into a mishmash of loud shock.

Another man sauntered in, with the same dark hair and beaked nose as Matthew's father and other brother. "Stop tormenting him, Mom. You promised

Elspeth you'd be nice and not scare Lila. You know that witch wants grandkids."

"Shut it. Marcus." Izzy dropped her frown and giggled. "Sorry, couldn't resist. You both look so serious. I had to do something to break the ice."

Izzy grabbed Lila by the hand and dragged her into a large kitchen with a Chinese-food-laden table. "Hope you're hungry."

"I could eat," Lila admitted.

"Right. Lila, you're next to me. I don't care where the rest of you rabble sit."

A slim man with the same dark hair and hooked nose, but green eyes like his mother's, looked up as the women entered the room. "I'm starving, can we eat yet?" He considered Lila over the top of his thick book. "About time you got here. Mom's been crazy planning this lunch."

Matthew held out Lila's chair and sat on one side of her, his mother on the other. He introduced his family as they filed in. "You've met my dad, Ed. My mom is Izzy." He pointed at the first brother they'd encountered. "The bearded caveman is my eldest brother, Lucas. The grumpy one is my middle brother, Marcus. And the one with his nose in a book is Owen."

"And Matthew's my baby." His mother blew her

youngest son a kiss. "Now, Elspeth gave us a list of all your favorite foods. So dig in."

Lila watched as the men shoveled food onto their plates, piling them high. She leaned over to Matthew. "Does your mother starve them? They're storing more food away than Holly does."

"My family gets serious about food. How our moods are when we wake up is pretty much decided by how good our food is."

If one wanted to take this reaper family down, all they had to do was burn a meal or two. Lila filed that weakness away for future mayhem and concentrated on catching up in the food stakes.

After consuming a large part of the Chinese banquet, Ed leaned back and focused on Lila. "I hear you have more bodies in town?"

"When isn't there a body count in Point Muse?" Lila pushed her plate away, appetite satisfied.

"Point Muse sounds like a fascinating place. Hopefully, you'll have the wedding there and we'll get to stay awhile." Izzy blinked wide eyes innocently at Lila and Matthew.

"Mother," Matthew warned his mom and the rest of the table erupted into laughter.

"I'll behave." Izzy rolled her eyes at her son's dramatics.

Ed ignored his wife's antics. "Elspeth thinks her nemesis is involved. It's a conspiracy to bring the Harrow family down."

"Elspeth also believes in alien abductions. Someone's definitely killing people connected to the Church of the Repentant Creature. Whether or not it's her nemesis, I have no clue."

"And the killer is targeting Lila," Matthew added.

"Who do you think it is, Lila?" Owen, the quietest of the Grims, spoke up.

"Elspeth and my cousin, Xandie, are positive the Devlins are involved." Lila toyed with her cutlery. "I've no doubt Delilah's involved in something nefarious, but I'm beginning to wonder if someone else is responsible for the bodies."

Matthew whooped. "About time you saw the light."

"Ex...cuse me?" Lila narrowed her eyes on her boyfriend. "Let's not crow too soon. You're just swayed by the fluttering of eyelashes and sugar-filled desserts. You're not exactly a neutral party."

"I told you, the Devlins aren't involved. At least, the twins aren't," he amended his statement.

Ed thumped the table. "Boy, don't sass your girl.

You'll have a much better sleep if you're in the bed, not on the couch."

His brothers roared with laughter and ribbed the youngest sibling about sleeping on the couch.

"I can't stand you lot any more. I need girl time." Izzy jumped up and dragged Lila with her. "I'll give Lila the tour while you drop your souls off in containment, Matthew. Behave, boys." She guided Lila out of the kitchen. "Now we can get some peace and quiet." She tucked her arm through Lila's and strolled down a light-filled corridor.

"Are they always like that?"

"Loud and painful?" Izzy nodded. "That's them on their best behavior, sadly."

"They're the same as my family. We'll squabble and tease, but when a threat looms, we have each other's backs."

"Exactly." Izzy opened the door to a large library. "This is Owen's domain. He's a bookworm and our research guy."

"My cousin, Xandie, would love this. She's the Librarian to the supernatural Great Library of Alexandria."

"I'm not a book girl. I'm more action oriented." Izzy kept strolling until she came to another door. "This is where Lucas mainly operates. He's weapons and training." Izzy opened the door to a massive gym with a glass room full of different types of weapons. "He's a doer too, and our muscle." Izzy closed the door and pointed to another. "That's Marcus's office. He deals with strategy and planning. But he's boring. You need to see where Ed and I work." Izzy dragged Lila up to a solid metal door. She placed a hand over a glass plate screwed into the wall next to the door, which then swung open with a musical chime.

"Nice security."

"Owen's a tech head as well as our bookworm. He designed all the security." Izzy swept an arm around the room. "This is our containment room."

A large vault sat at the end of the room. The rest of the space was decorated with low-slung tables and chairs, and a large wooden bookcase which sat on the opposite side. Thick carpets covered a solid concrete floor and a pool table sat in the middle of the room. "Seems nice."

"This is where we contain any souls collected until they can be processed onto the next plane. Plus, Ed and I like to get away from the kids and relax in here with a game of pool. It's great, we can lock them out. But the whining after is pitiful." Izzy opened the vault with another hand scan.

Lila stepped forward to get a better look. Row

upon row of shelving filled the vault. And each shelf housed a clear, stoppered bottle with glowing liquid in it. "Souls?"

"Yep." Izzy patted the vault tenderly. "This old girl is top-notch in soul retrieval and containment technology. We couldn't do our job without her." Izzy backed up and made sure Lila was clear, locked the vault down again. She spun on the spot and put her hands to her hips. "Now. Woman to woman. Mathew's the sweetest and most caring of all my boys. But he still inherited his thick head from his father. If you feel those Devlin girls are up to no good—whatever it is—*they probably are.*"

"There's no proof they killed anyone."

"I'm not talking about murders. I'm talking about flirty shenanigans with my Matthew. You can trust him but he's not going to see any flirty manipulation unless it hits him on the head. You need to take charge and show him who's boss."

"Oh, there's definitely flirty shenanigans happening."

Izzy wrinkled her nose and punched a fist into the palm of her hand. "Take charge and establish your territory."

"Whose territory are you raiding now, Mom?" Matthew strolled in and headed for the vault.

Lila cleared her throat. "No territories. Your Mom's just taking me on a tour and explaining how your business works."

"Why don't I believe you?" Matthew stepped inside the vault for a few minutes before heading back out and locking it. He dusted his hands off. "All done. Now we can get to the sightseeing portion of our trip."

Taking Izzy up on her advice, Lila cleared her throat. "About that."

Matthew looked worried. "Spit it out, Harrow."

"I've got a change of plans for us." Lila winked at a beaming Izzy. Matthew would hate her idea, but it was time she tracked down some of Delilah's victims.

She had to know just what Elspeth's nemesis was capable of...

FOURTEEN

"This is not what I had in mind when I suggested sightseeing."

"I'm hungry. I thought a trip to a bakery here in Portland would satisfy my hunger." Lila smirked at her boyfriend.

"Stop smiling. I feel like you're about to order a hit on me. And as for the bakery, you can't tell me the fact it's owned by an ex of Delilah's isn't the main reason you're here?"

Lila dropped the act. "I admit nothing. Now let's eat." She pushed the door open to the small bakery. The smell of fresh bread wafted over Lila, and she inhaled deeply. There was something about freshly cooked baked goods that made her day.

"Come on in, girl. Can't get fed if you stand on

the doorstep." A short, red-cheeked woman with twinkling eyes waved Lila in.

Matthew grabbed the smallest table near the front windows. "Do your baker bonding, but don't forget to order a slice of red velvet cake for me."

"What can I get you, dear?"

"A slice of red velvet cake for the hangry man and I'd like some information." Lila smiled at the suddenly suspicious woman. "I'm a baker too."

The woman served up a slice of red velvet cake and handed it off to a young woman who placed it in front of the reaper.

"What kind of information are you after? I don't hand out my recipes, especially not to another baker."

"Delilah Devlin."

The woman's face hardened to stone. "If you're a friend of that woman's, don't let the door hit you on the way out."

"Whoa." Lila held up a hand. "Delilah Devlin and my grandmother are mortal enemies. Delilah and her granddaughters, Ruby and Rose, have moved to our town and opened a dessert bakery opposite *my* bakery. I just want to know about the family."

"The twins." The woman's face softened. "Those girls are too good for the Devlins."

Lila leaned against the counter. "Can you tell me anything about them?"

The baker reached behind her back and untied her apron. "Luce, I'm taking a break," she hollered at the young woman who'd delivered Matthew's cake. "Let's keep your man company while he tastes my cake. He can give me his opinion later."

At least the woman hadn't thrown her out of the bakery at the mention of Delilah's name.

"Those poor girls are still mixed up with that woman, I take it?"

"Their grandmother, Delilah? She sold her store to stake the twins in their new bakery. She's living above the shop in an apartment."

The baker snorted. "That woman just can't let go." She held a calloused hand out. "I'm Louella, I run this bakery now."

Lila shook her hand, while Matthew nodded at the woman. "I'm Lila Harrow and this is Matthew Grim. I thought one of Delilah's exes owned the bakery?"

"My idiot brother, Hamish. This is a family bakery and he almost bankrupted it for that she-devil."

"Delilah drained his finances?"

"She has expensive taste, and my moron younger

brother couldn't say no." Louella sighed. "In his defense, it's hard to say no to her. I took over when our debtors started calling. We're finally making money again and he's much happier out back baking in the kitchen."

Matthew sighed and pushed the empty plate to the side. "That was delicious."

"Not so hangry now, Grim?"

"I'm taking your advice, Lila. You always tell me that sugar makes everything better."

Louella slapped at her thigh, let out a sharp burst of laughter and pointed at Grim. "You better listen to your girl, she's always right."

"Speaking of bakers." Lila leaned forward. "What about the twins? They worked here for a while, I heard."

"Those girls worked hard and loved anything to do with the kitchen. No matter what I threw at them, they flew through it with a smile. I think they were happy to get away from their family's business, truth be told."

"Delilah's potion business?"

"Yeah. The whole family worked in the store. Even the girls' parents. But the twins hated working there. When Delilah started seeing my brother, she introduced them to the bakery. They spent every moment they could here. My brother started showing them recipes. Those two have a gift with sugar and loved making desserts. I felt sorry for them."

Why feel sorry for someone who had mad skills in baking? You'd think a baker would applaud it. Lila hadn't realized she'd spoken aloud until Louella answered.

"Their family hated the time they spent here. One afternoon, their mother turned up. What a piece of work." Louella grimaced. "Over-plucked and snooty to boot. She ranted how the girls were wasting their time and they should be working in the family business. Contributing to the family coffers. She yanked them out of here quicksmart."

Against her will, Lila felt sorry for the twins. She had no clue what she would've done if her family had stopped her baking or opening her shop.

"Feeling bad now, aren't you?" Matthew nudged Lila.

"Shut it, Grim."

"That's how I felt too. I wanted to hate those kids because of their family, but those two are different from the rest."

"What about Delilah? What did she think about the twins baking?"

"I can't stand that woman, but I'll say this. She supported those girls and made sure they had whatever they needed. Still doesn't mean I like her."

Ditto for Lila. "Thanks for your time, Louella."

The baker pushed away from the table. "Happy to help a fellow baker. The girls have good hearts, but Devlin blood still flows through their veins. They mean well, but sometimes their family's a bad influence. Watch your backs." Louella nodded and headed back behind the counter.

Matthew finally spoke up. "Happy now? Can we sightsee yet?"

"Soon." One more address to look up then they could head for home. Hopefully, to a quiet, chaos-free Point Muse.

A bell rang shrilly as Lila opened the door to *Potions-A-Go-Go*. Delilah Devlin's old potion store.

"This place gives me the creeps." Matthew shuddered theatrically.

"Hey, I'm a drama llama, not you." Lila nudged her boyfriend but couldn't deny his words. Aunt Winifred's potion and candle store was light and welcoming. Wonderful smells permeated the store, and it was as clean as a whistle. Lila ran a finger along a shelf, and it came away black. She wiped her dirty digit on the back of Matthew's shirt.

"Lila," Matthew complained.

"You just protected me from death by no-housekeeper. Aren't you proud?"

"Words fail me."

Snorting, Lila carefully marched further into the store. The shelves around her held a hodgepodge of potion bottles filled with different colored mixtures. Cobwebs draped themselves in the corner of the store and overhead a flickering light glowed dimly.

"What's your poison?" A gravelly low voice echoed from the back of the store. A hulking, grey-haired man loomed behind the counter.

"Just information." Matthew took charge and stepped in front of Lila.

Her big protector. Lila bit back a smile. She was perfectly able to take care of herself, but it was kind of nice, occasionally, when someone else stepped up.

"Information will cost you."

"Delilah Devlin." Matthew's words hit the man behind the counter like a sledgehammer.

He reared back and thumped a grimy hand down on the counter. "That name gets you nothing here. Do you understand me? Nothing. Get out of my shop." He turned his back on Lila and Matthew and disappeared through a back door.

"Well, that was more the reaction I expected when we mentioned Delilah at the bakery." The potion seller's reaction was exactly the way Lila's grandmother had reacted when she'd seen Delilah… With extreme prejudice.

"Sorry. Her name's like a red flag for him. Davros will calm down eventually, but you might want to leave while he's out back," a small voice said from behind them.

Lila swung around. A tiny woman with a dirt-encrusted duster stood near a window display. "We didn't mean to upset him, but we're after information on Delilah Devlin."

The woman placed her duster on a shelf. "Delilah's a sore subject for Davros."

"Ex-boyfriend?" Matthew asked.

"Goodness, no." The woman giggled for a moment before calming. "Davros is the only male I know immune to her charms, but he's a gambler and Delilah likes poker."

"Let me guess. She cheated him and ran off?" Sounds like something Elspeth would do. Maybe the nemeses weren't so different after all.

"Kind of. They played poker and Davros won.

Delilah only had the shop to offer. He thought it might be a good money making gig.”

“Except?”

“She gave him the deed after she’d already sold it to somebody else and banked the check. She did a midnight flit and Davros turned up the next day to his brand-new shop that somebody else had already taken possession of. It was a bloodbath.” The woman shivered. “Eventually, Davros gained the upper hand and the other owner left, swearing black and blue he’d get revenge on both Delilah and Davros.”

“And did he?” Maybe Lila had another suspect to add to her list.

“Not that I’m aware of. As soon as he left here, the man was nabbed for tax evasion. Turns out he’d actually been Delilah’s very silent partner and she left him to carry the can. Davros moved in and here we are now.” The woman sneezed and wiped her nose. “Sorry. Delilah wasn’t known for her housekeeping. I tried, but it was too hard for one person to keep up.”

“You worked for Delilah?” *Now they were getting somewhere.*

“The only employee besides her family.” She shuddered. “Bunch of barracudas, the lot of them. Except for the twins.” She brightened. “The girls were lovely. And Delilah was always entertaining, of course."

Matthew cleared his throat. "I heard that Delilah had a certain reputation."

"She liked men and money and it got her into trouble. The whole family was like that, except the twins. They only cared about baking. And they weren't malicious like the rest of the family. Delilah's okay, but the parents and the other family hangers-on? They weren't nice. They kinda played fast and loose with the potions."

"What do you mean?" Matthew frowned, trying to puzzle the other woman's words out.

"The ingredients in most of the potions weren't exactly ethically or legally sourced. PIG raided the store at least once a week. But nothing stuck. Poor Davros had to throw a lot of stock out. He decided to keep me on because I can mix potions. We're cleaning and overhauling the entire store. All above board," the woman proclaimed proudly.

Lila decided to take a chance and asked a question of her own. "Did Delilah have any enemies that stood out?"

The potion shop employee snorted. "Too long a list to remember. Now that you mention it, there was one woman. She stalked Delilah for ages, even protested outside the store."

"Do you know why?"

"Delilah dated the husband while he was still married. He became obsessed with her. The wife lost it when he left her. Not long after, Delilah broke it off and he had a heart attack and died. The wife blamed Delilah. She spread rumors about the store, laid complaints with PIG, and picketed us. She was a real menace. Then the old girl just disappeared. Delilah was relieved the loony tune had finally given up."

Delilah definitely inspired strong emotions in people. "Did you happen to catch the scorned woman's name? Description?"

"She was plump with long straight, mousy brown hair, I think. Her name was Sherry something. I can't remember her last name, sorry."

Lila smiled. "That's okay. You've been a big help. I hope you get the potions store up and running soon."

The lady beamed. "Thank you. Take care if you're dealing with the Devlin family. They're kind of slippery."

"I have experience in dealing with slippery characters. Thanks again." Lila waved and strolled outside.

"Got enough information yet?" Matthew wound an arm around Lila's waist as they headed back to the car.

"Enough to start getting a picture." Lila pursed her lips. "The more background I get, the more I need to work all the angles out."

"Sleuthing's hard."

"So is dealing with Elspeth on a warpath. You know what I'm going to say next?" Lila raised an eyebrow.

"We need to get back to Point Muse." Matthew sighed.

"It's okay, reaper." Lila patted Matthew's cheek. "Next time, I promise we'll spend longer in Portland, and you can show me all the sights." For now, they needed to get back home and catch a killer.

Before the killer caught them.

FIFTEEN

"I came back for that?" Lila slapped yesterday's Point Muse Chronicle on her bakery kitchen bench. "That sneaky newshound waited until I was away for the day to write that trash?"

"Don't they say any publicity is good publicity?" Holly leaned over her cup of tea and inhaled.

"Stop sniffing your drink and support me. You're family. You're supposed to be here for me in my hour of need," Lila wailed.

"There, there, it'll be fine." Holly took a sip of tea and sighed contentedly.

"Lots of energy was put into that affirmation. What's wrong with you today?"

"I'm over the drama of Point Muse. I need a holiday."

"Holidays are overrated. I had a day trip and look what I came home to. That." Lila grabbed the newspaper.

"Percy Hague might as well have proclaimed me the killer. He's ruined my reputation and business." She threw the newspaper across the kitchen and accidentally hit Matthew in the face as he entered.

"Whoa." The reaper snapped a hand up and snagged the newspaper. "Everything okay?"

"No," Lila moaned. "Percy Hague wrote a hatchet job about me in the Point Muse Chronicle. I'm finished."

"Pretty sure it's not that bad. Who reads newspapers anyway? It's the digital age."

Fixing her boyfriend with a withering stare, Lila increased her pacing. "It's Point Muse. Digital doesn't always work and the oldies in town like to read newspapers while they sip a hot drink from my bakery... At least they did until they read that article."

"Percival Hague will regret he ever crossed me." Elspeth blew into the kitchen, a whirling dervish in a neon green jogging suit with a clashing cascade of curly pink curls.

Colin wobbled in and collapsed, spread eagle on the floor. "Feed me," he moaned pathetically. "She power walked here; I'm dying from starvation. She wouldn't even feed me tuna this morning."

Lila shuddered and backed away from the flatulent-ridden pug, just to be safe.

"We're keeping that weapon under wraps until we need it. Which might be sooner rather than later if that hack reporter doesn't rehire me."

Holly stared mournfully at her now empty teacup. "Didn't he fire you from the food critic job ages ago?"

"He didn't mean it. But this time he cut off my tab at the Santos Bros Pizzeria. He's gone too far now." Shadows wreathed Elspeth's feet like a set of woolly feet warmers.

"Percy owns the Chronicle. Why would he cut your pizza tab off? What's that got to do with him?"

Elspeth sniffed. "I like to have ambience when I write up my food critiques. And, of course, I need to keep my energy levels up with food. Harvey Santos always puts the pizza on my tab and bills the paper."

"Harvey's been trying to get into Elspeth's granny pants for decades." Holly held out her teacup. "More," she begged Lila.

"Nope. You're cut off for not being supportive."

Matthew held the newspaper out to Lila. "Your

lethal projectile was about an article the reporter wrote?"

Lila snatched the newspaper and waved it at the reaper. "Apparently, the food at the Devlins' grand opening was a cut above the normal fare offered in Point Muse. And the Devlins' bakery brings class and dignity to the town which is sorely lacking."

"It's not like he names your bakery."

Lila snatched her cousin's teacup away. "No more caffeine for you. It's not just those comments. Our friendly newshound then goes on to mention the devilish Devlins are being subjected to biased persecution based on their family name by a certain unsavory element in Point Muse society." Lila slapped the newspaper. "How do you like them baked goods?"

Elspeth sniffed. "The only good thing about that article is the unsavory element bit. I like unsavory."

"You do know he's referring to you, right?" Holly raised an eyebrow at her grandmother.

"Like I said. That's the best bit of the article." Elspeth stomped to the center of the room. Shadows twirled around her legs like a mini tornado. "It's time we stormed the bastion of the written word in Point Muse and take that evil tab destroyer down." Elspeth pumped a fist into the air. "Who's with me?" she roared.

"Will you feed me?" Colin whined.

"Can I get a top-up yet?"

Lila screeched at her cousin, "I told you. Stop asking for tea."

"Okay. Let's all calm down before we storm the Chronicle." Matthew held up his hands.

"Don't you calm me down, Matthew Grim." Lila stormed up to Elspeth and yanked her by her arm. "Let's go, Elspeth. I have a full head of steam and I plan to explode all over the reporter's office."

"Solidarity, sister." Elspeth smirked and snapped her fingers. "Let's go, Colin. I'm sure Percy will have snacks. If not, you'll have to hold him hostage until he feeds you."

"Look what the wicked witch dragged in." The receptionist for the Point Muse Chronicle wrinkled her nose like she'd smelt something bad.

"Don't give me attitude, Macy. I'm at my limit. I want to see Percy, right now." Lila slammed her hands on her hips. "And I'm willing to set Elspeth on him if he won't talk to me."

"Now, now, no need to get nasty." The brassy redhead capped her nail polish and blew gently on her pale pink painted nails. "As it happens, Mr. Hague does have two appointments with him currently." Macy grimaced. "Those two are all over him. Sickening to watch, truly sickening."

She sniffed, and then smiled slowly as she took in Elspeth and Colin standing behind Lila. "You know what? I think it would be perfect timing if you spoke to Percy right now." The redhead winked. "Go right ahead, Harrows. Go forth and cause menace." Macy waved them through.

Righteous anger bubbling, Lila marched into Percy's office and flung the door open, surprising Ruby Devlin, who lounged on an upright chair, and Rose, who'd plastered herself against the red-faced Percy. "Back off, Devlins. I gotta have words with a cursed reporter."

"I'm not cursed."

"You will be, Percival Hague." Elspeth pointed an accusing finger at the blushing young man. "Why do you have red lipstick on your cheek?"

"I.. Um..." Percy ran a finger around the collar of his shirt.

"Your mother would be disappointed." Elspeth shook her head gravely. "We'll all need to cleanse ourselves and purify our souls." Elspeth lowered her head as if deep in thought but cracked one eye open to see Percy's reaction.

He cleared his throat. "There's no need to speak to my mother." He blushed as he glanced at Ruby and Rose and straightened his askew glasses. "Ruby and Rose are special. But you're right, this is a professional environment and we should act more businesslike."

Rose nodded. "We were just thanking Percy for that lovely article he wrote about our grand opening yesterday."

"Of course you are," Lila drawled. She threw the newspaper she clutched at Percy. "Thanks for nothing, Hague. Way to torpedo a sinking ship. I thought Point Muse residents were supposed to stick together and not get distracted by fluttering eyelashes and sweet smiles?"

"Now hang on." Ruby jumped up from her chair.

Elspeth jerked her head up and grabbed Colin, pointing him at the twins. "No sudden movements or the pug goes off."

"Ah, Elspeth? Queen of my life?" Colin whispered.

"Shush, sweetie. You're my ultimate threat."

Colin cleared his throat. "About that? You haven't fed me for an hour. I'm not primed to blow yet."

"For Hecate's sake! You just can't rely on a good evil minion these days." Elspeth deposited Colin on the floor. "I guess I'll have to rely on my natural wickedness then."

"Now, Elspeth, I fired you weeks ago. You can't expect me to keep your tab going at the pizzeria when you weren't even an employee."

"Can't I? Can't I, Percival Hague?" Elspeth widened her eyes. "Wait until I have a little chat with your mother about your goings on. You know she calls me once a month for updates. Have I got some doozies to tell her this time."

Percy ran his hand through his hair. "All right. Fine. You can reopen your tab again."

"Nice doing business with you, kid." Colin winked at the reporter. "Got snacks in that desk?"

"Seriously? That's all you have to say, Elspeth? What about the article? Are you even going to stand up for your granddaughter?" Lila demanded as she caught Elspeth trying to sneak out of the room.

Sighing, Elspeth turned. "Right. Forgot about that other reason."

Lila turned back to Percy. "Are you trying to ruin

me? You put down my food, then insinuate I'm trying to persecute the Devlins."

"Look, Lila, I'm a reporter. I have to stay neutral and report things as I see them."

"Neutral?" Lila stomped around the desk and rubbed the lipstick mark from Percy's cheek. I think this is called hypocrisy, Mr. Hague."

Ruby stepped around the reporter. "See here, Lila Harrow. Your family has done nothing but make us feel unwelcome since we arrived."

"It was my food that was sabotaged first, not yours. But I don't see that written about, except to say it's substandard to the Devlins'. And now look, the same reporter who wrote that is kissing up to the competition."

"Well." Percy held a hand up as Rose joined her sister in glaring at the Harrows. "To be fair, Lila has a point. For once."

Lila grimaced but let the reporter continue.

"In light of my growing relationship with the Devlin's and the fact that the issues around the events of the last few days haven't been completely explained. I'm willing to write an updated and impartial article detailing the events leading up to the Devlins grand opening. The article will go in tomorrow's issue. How's that for a compromise?"

Lila sniffed. "Thank you, Percy." She frowned. "What about today's issue?"

"Too late. It's already gone out. We featured a story about Janice Hagar being poisoned and that she's now in a coma at Point Muse hospital."

Dread rolled over Lila. The killer would know they'd failed. They might attempt a second run at poor Janice, like they'd done with Elaine. "Hecate's executioner. Percy, do you realize you might be signing Janice's death warrant? The killer will know they failed."

Percy paled, and the twins crowded closer. "I didn't realize. I... It's already gone out, both digitally and physically. I can't recall the newspaper."

Lila grabbed Colin and heaved him onto her hip. "We need to get to the hospital now."

Elspeth rubbed her hands. "Give up your bakery van keys. I can get us there in a flash."

Sadly, the way Elspeth drove, she was probably right. Lila flicked the keys over to her grandmother.

"Have at them, race car granny."

"Have I told you about the time I worked as a rally car driver?"

"No. But I'm sure you're about to."

For once, Lila didn't mind the wicked witch's cackle as they raced to her van. Sometimes a girl just needed a wicked witch on her side...

SIXTEEN

"I can't believe you nearly ran that man over," Lila panted as she raced through the hospital corridor.

"His mobility scooter was in the way. I need to get me one of those. A hot pink one to match my little moped. You can ride one and we could be twinsies."

"Only in my nightmares."

"Could you gals hold up? That butter puff I ate in the van wasn't enough to stand up to cardio," Colin huffed next to Elspeth as they hot footed it through the hospital.

Lila skidded to a stop next to the nurses' station.

"I need Janice Hager's room."

A young brunette nurse lifted her head. "Are you family?"

"No. I'm a baker."

"Unless you're family, you can't visit her."

"But I'm here to stop her murder."

"Ms. Hager has already been poisoned but is responding nicely and will be perfectly safe in Point Muse hospital." The young woman crossed her arms and stepped out from the nurse's station. "Do I need to call security?"

"Let me handle this." The Harrow matriarch smiled benignly at the nurse. "You're new here, aren't you?"

With the exception of one older woman, the rest of the nurses vacated the station at a run.

"I am new to Point Muse, but rules are rules."

"Of course. Of course. But you see, my granddaughter's trying to help. Surely you can tell us the room number?"

"No. As I said, family only." The nurse stubbornly refused to budge.

Shadows squirmed around the nurses' station like a dark ring of snakes and computers began to emit high-pitched whines as they flicked off and on.

"Room 30. End of the corridor, turn left. It's the last room."

The young woman spun to her colleague. "Why

did you tell them? They aren't family. It's against regulations."

Yanking the younger nurse back behind the station, the woman shot Elspeth an apologetic smile. "She just transferred in and it's her first day. We haven't had a chance to explain about the Harrows yet."

"She better learn quick." Elspeth twirled her finger and the shadows swirled around one more time, before disappearing back under Elspeth's feet. She looked at Lila. "What are you waiting for? Get to the church mouse. I'll wait here and make sure Braun knows where to go when he arrives."

Taking Elspeth at her word, Lila bolted down the corridor, turned and then headed for the last room. The door stood slightly ajar, and she just made out a white coated form standing close to the bed. Lila screeched as she smacked the door open. "Oi." The figure in the doctor's coat with a cap and a surgical mask froze, then dropped the pillow they'd been holding over Janice's head, and raced through a connecting door on the other side of the room.

Making sure Janice still breathed, Lila ran for the door. But the room next to the church secretary was completely empty. She searched the corridor and spotted a white-coated figure disappearing in the opposite direction of the nurses' station.

"I might be a baker and lack Elspeth's stamina, but I'm Harrow stubborn." Lila took off after the mysterious figure. Braun would arrive any minute for the Janice protection detail. Lila just had to catch the killer. She poured on a burst of speed. "Stop right there," she yelled, but the killer ignored her and surged through a set of double doors that swung closed as Lila reached them.

"Rude much? Aren't you supposed to hold doors open for a lady?" Lila opened the doors herself and stepped into chaos. She pulled to a stop and searched the room. Parents and babies filled every seat and countless figures in doctors' coats milled around the room. Lila found the nearest nurse. "What's going on?"

"Someone called and reported a bright pox infection. We need to get all those under two years of age in Point Muse vaccinated today. Thankfully, we just got a new order of the vaccine yesterday."

"What a coincidence." Smart killer, hiding in plain sight and two steps ahead of Lila. "Did a doctor come in here a few seconds ago? They would've been in a rush."

The nurse snorted. "There are doctors every-where. And it's a hospital, everyone's in a rush."

"Thanks anyway." Lila wandered through the crowd, scanning for anyone that looked hot and flustered. Unfortunately, on vaccination day, everyone, including the babies, looked hot.

"Needle in a haystack," Lila moaned. She marched out through the double glass front doors onto a large, grassed area in front of a packed parking lot.

"Sneaky, sneaky." This killer wasn't putting a foot wrong. Made it very hard for a sleuth to catch a killer.

"Let me guess. One of Elspeth's hexes went astray, and the poor innocent victim ended up in the hospital." Delilah Devlin strolled through the parking lot toward Lila, with Ruby, Rose, and her poodle, Kali.

Rose grimaced. "Sorry, when she heard about Janice, she insisted we come to the hospital and check on her ourselves."

"You know what it's like. Can't talk them out of anything and you can't say no, or they'll hex you." Rose shrugged.

"I hear you." What a shame Lila had to agree with her mortal enemies.

"I hear you decided to visit some of my old haunts in Portland when you met the in-laws. Got a nice ear-full of gossip, did you?" Delilah sneered.

"Would it surprise you to know you aren't universally loved? Your old employee still likes you though. But the new owner wanted to throw us out as soon as he heard your name."

"Dear Davros. A good poker player, but such a temper." She shook her head. "How's the old shop going?"

"They're cleaning and fumigating right now. Apparently, they had to throw out all the old stock as the majority of it wasn't exactly aboveboard."

"These things happen."

"And I spoke to Louella at the bakery," Lila addressed the twins. "I think she misses you both. She had nothing but good things to say about you guys. Not Delilah, of course."

Ruby blushed. "Louella's an amazing baker and has such a light touch with cakes."

"Do you have any other dirt on me?"

"Only that you have a lot of enemies. Most of your family's kind of mean and some woman stalked you because you stole her husband."

Delilah's eyes flashed. "I genuinely cared about Alvin. His wife had mental issues and it wasn't my fault he died of a heart attack after we broke up."

"It's never your fault, deadly Devlin. Is it?" Elspeth strolled out.

Kali, Delilah's snooty poodle, growled low and bared her teeth when Elspeth and Colin joined the group.

"Hey, babe. Don't be hating on my Queen. Look at your own house." Colin twitched his nose at the white poodle, who was the size of a small pony.

"Your little baker's been digging in my past, Harrow. I should report the harassment to Zachy."

"Zachy is too busy dealing with another murder attempt." Elspeth shifted until she stood in front of her granddaughter. "And you're right here at the hospital as it happened. What a surprise."

"Circumstantial. But while we're here, we might as well check in with Zach. Let him know how far the Harrows are willing to go to persecute the Devlin family." Delilah stepped to within touching distance of Elspeth, then sneezed on her. "So sorry. The Eau du Desperation clogged my nasal passages." Smiling, Delilah shoved her way past Elspeth and into the hospital.

"Sorry." Ruby mouthed to Lila as the twins trotted behind their grandmother.

Kali strutted by Colin and slapped his face as she passed.

"Where I come from, sweetheart, that's called foreplay, you know?" Colin sighed as the poodle ignored him. "Why is it the mean ones are the most attractive?"

"Fact of life, pug. That poodle is as nasty as her owner. I'd stay away," Elspeth growled. "She had the last word. I hate it when she does that."

"What was that sneeze about?"

"She probably laced me with another hex." Elspeth grinned. "The fun is working out which one."

Both women were as bad as the other. Lila needed to get back into the hospital and let Braun know about the second murder attempt. A small meow snagged Lila's attention as a tiny grey cat prowled up next to her. "What a cutie." She bent over and scratched behind the animal's ear.

"I wouldn't touch that mangy mouser. You know that old saying. You lay down with cats, you get up with fleas." Colin took a sidestep away from the feline.

Another meow sounded from behind a car and a black cat stepped out and strolled toward Elspeth.

The cat pulled up short in front of the Harrow matriarch and rubbed against her jogging suit-covered leg.

"Step away from the feline. You don't know where that plague carrier's been." Colin shuddered.

More meowing sounded as two different colored animals stalked Elspeth from one side.

Lila dropped her hand and took a prudent step closer to the hospital. All the cats ignored her and focused on Elspeth. "I think you might have a problem." Lila pointed to another group of cats zeroing in on Elspeth from the other side of the parking lot.

"That rat fink." Elspeth took a large step and the cats jolted forward.

"Care to educate the rest of us who don't speak Elspeth?"

"That Devlin sneak. I worked out what the hex was." She pointed to the cats. "That evil woman knows I can't stand cats. She love-hexed them and set them loose on me. Sneaky."

"On that thought, why don't you stay here while I update Braun." Lila edged around the synchronized purring felines.

"I'm with you, baker babe. That purring and staring scares the pug out of me." Colin hugged Lila's leg as they backed up to the hospital's entrance, never taking their eyes away from the crowd of waiting animals.

"Lila Marie Harrow! Don't you dare leave me alone with these things."

"Sorry, Gran. On a timetable here. Got things to do." Namely, update Braun then head to the church and have a little chat with Pastor Ezekiel Moss. The church had their weekly meeting with a catered dinner tomorrow night. Lila had questions she wanted answered before the killer had another opportunity to strike.

"Lila? Please don't leave me," Elspeth wailed as her granddaughter and pug deserted her without a backward glance.

Sometimes, a girl had to judge the situation and know when to retreat.

And this was one of those days.

SEVENTEEN

"I don't think I'm the right person for covert activities."

"Aunt Winifred, you're the perfect person for this job." Lila ducked and dragged her aunt around the side of the church.

"Remind me again, why?" Winifred hugged the side of the church.

"Because you left my bowls here from the last church meeting and we're just here to pick them up before I have to cater the next one. That's a valid reason if anyone bounces us."

Winifred cleared her throat. "About the next church meeting, I have some bad news."

"Can it wait until after our spying?" Lila popped up on her toes and peered through the window. The

Church of the Repentant Creatures was a good-sized, weatherboard church that stood by itself on a small plot of land at the edge of town. A heavily wooded area owned by the town backed onto the church property. Serenity was the key word, perfect for spying on a playboy pastor.

"Lila. I must tell you something. Don't hate me?"

Winifred clasped Lila to her chest and rushed her words out. "The church decided to offer the Devlins the catering for the next church meeting. They want to be fair. I'm sorry I didn't tell you earlier, but I was trying to find the right time."

"And spying on the pastor is the right time?"

"I couldn't hold it in any longer," Winifred admitted.

"Can you let me go now? My oxygen's depleting." Lila tried to wiggle away from a large curl of Winifred's bright red hair which was currently trying to strangle her.

"Oops. Sorry." Winifred released Lila. "You don't seem too upset?"

"I'm not." And she honestly wasn't. The Devlins desserts were delicious, and they loved baking as much as Lila did. She was more worried about the impact on her bakery business, but the Harrows didn't own the town. If the twins wanted to set up shop here, they could. She didn't have to like the flirting or Delilah Devlin, but they had a right to be here... If they weren't killers.

"Oh sweetie. I'm so pleased with you." Winifred clapped her hands, delight evident on her face. "This is growth and, in a Harrow, that's a miracle."

"Okay, okay." Lila fought a blush and directed her aunt back to the task at hand. "Spying on the playboy pastor, remember?"

"Right." Grinning, Winifred wedged herself in next to Lila. "This is quite exciting, isn't it? No wonder Xandie and Holly enjoy it."

"Shush." Lila peered through the window and spotted Ezekiel pacing up and down the aisle.

"What's he doing?"

"Pacing. Looks like he's worried about something or waiting for someone."

The screeching of brakes in front of the church filled the air.

"I vote for meeting someone." Winifred wriggled closer to the window. "This is better than Witch Island on TV."

"Nothing's happened yet." Winifred needed to get out more. A door slammed at the front of the church and a familiar, skinny blonde on teetering heels, strutted into the church. "We need to get inside that church. We have to hear this conversation."

"Isn't that dangerous? We might get caught."

"We're only here for the bowls, remember? Let's head to the kitchen, we can hear better there." Lila crept around the side of the church to the back door that led into a small kitchen, with a restroom next to it. She tried the door handle and crowed silently as she let Winifred into the kitchen first.

"Oh, look. They've already washed and stacked your dishes up for us. How nice of them."

"Focus, Winifred." Lila cracked open the kitchen door a little. Ahead was a bare hallway which led past an office and out into the church.

"What do you want, Chastity?"

"How hard you sound, Zeke. Can't a wife meet her husband without the third-degree?"

Ezekiel and Chastity's voices floated clearly down to Lila and Winifred.

"Ex. We divorced."

"Oh, sweetie. Just because we divorced, doesn't mean I don't love you. I couldn't cope with all the church stuff. You know? It's intense."

Lila rolled her eyes. Chastity must be dead broke if she needed to work Ezekiel this hard.

The couple stopped talking for a few moments.

"What's happening? I can't hear anything."

"I think the barracuda has him in a lip lock," Lila whispered back to her aunt.

"That's enough, Chastity."

"Enough? How dare you push me away. None of those old church biddies can give you what I can."

"Drama? Bankruptcy?"

A sharp noise echoed through the church. It didn't take much to work out Chastity had slapped pastor playboy. Not exactly the way to hook your fish. But the ex-wife seemed to be the type to let her emotions, or at least her temper, rule her. Lila wiggled closer to the kitchen door. This conversation was just getting interesting.

"You'll regret rejecting me. Do you hear me?"

"What do you want to get out of my life?"

Chastity let out a theatrical laugh. "Bribery? How the mighty have fallen. What would your parishioners say if they saw you now?"

"We both know you need money. What will it take to get you out of my life permanently?"

"I thought the precious Moss family had cut off your access to the family money?"

"They have authorized one last withdrawal. After that, you get nothing but the lawyers."

"Wow. Pulling out all the stops to get rid of the

mouthy riff-raff," Chastity drawled. "Living on my own is expensive."

"There's a cheque for twenty thousand dollars on my desk. Take it and leave me alone."

"Leave you alone? Gladly." Chastity's voice changed, all the sweetness and light dissipated to reveal the venom underneath. "I'll happily leave this podunk town. Your churchgoers are dropping like flies. I want to get out of town before that cursed Harrow baker discovers my body. You're toxic, Ezekiel, and you don't even realize it."

"She doesn't like you much, dear," Aunt Winifred whispered.

"It's mutual." Lila drew back and closed the kitchen door until only a small gap remained. Just enough so she could see into the pastor's office.

"Take your money and go. The bad feelings in this town will leave with you. Everything will go back to normal."

"You always did like to bury your head in the sand and ignore the obvious. It's your funeral. And I mean that literally. I'm outta here." Chastity strutted down the hallway to Ezekiel's office.

Lila watched as the gold-digger glanced around the room, snatched the cheque up, and with a satisfied grunt, shoved it into her bra. She carefully eased the desk drawer open and rifled through until she found what she was looking for. A wad of cash secured with a red rubber band. Smiling widely, Chastity turned and headed back through the church.

"Quick. We need to follow her." Lila scuttled out the kitchen door and back around the side of the church to the empty lot where she'd hidden her bakery van.

Winifred hurried up to the van and clambered in. "Why are we following Chastity?"

"Because she's bad news and very, very greedy."

"You think she might be at risk?"

"Greed is a deadly sin. So that would be a big fat yes." Lila waited for Chastity's bright red sports car to flash past. She eased the van onto the road and kept a respectable distance between the two vehicles.

"That poor pastor had to pay off his ex-wife, just for a little peace?"

"She's a piece of work. They both are. He let the situation go on for far too long. He enabled her issues."

"Why, Lila. That sounds very insightful."

"Hester likes to watch all these daytime talk shows. You pick up the lingo after a while."

Lila concentrated on Chastity's tail lights. The

woman had a lead foot. Amazing Braun hadn't arrested the woman for speeding yet.

Chastity raced through Point Muse and headed out of town toward the highway. The little sports car had just passed Point Muse Academy when the car swerved erratically from side to side.

"What is wrong with that woman?" Lila slowed down to a crawl as the sports car jerked to the left and almost ran off the road.

"Aunt Winifred? I think we have a problem." Lila braked sharply as the car in front veered to the opposite side and then spun around ninety degrees and surged off the side of the road. Its nose slammed into one of the thick trees that lined the roadside.

Wrenching her van off to the side of the road, Lila braked to a stop. "Take the van and head to the Academy. Get them to call Braun and the healers, asap."

"On it." With a speed that belied her plump curves. Winifred climbed into the driver's seat. "Be careful, Lila."

"Always, Auntie." Lila blew Winifred a kiss and ran to the crumpled car. Chastity's windscreen had shattered, and glass lay sprinkled everywhere. The driver's door hung at a drunken angle as Lila wormed her way next to the open door and peered into the car. Chastity lay in a crumpled heap. The seatbelt had obviously saved her from going through her own windscreen, but she'd been tossed around and lay slumped, unconscious.

The injured woman's chest rose slowly. She'd survived the crash. "I don't like you, Chastity. But no one deserves to die on the side of the road by themselves. Hopefully, Braun's quick with the healers."

Chastity groaned and twitched, not fully conscious. Her clenched hand slipped to the side, the fingers relaxing. A wad of cash rolled out and exposed the rawness of Chastity's hand. Oozing blisters covered the palm. Portions of skin had peeled away, exposing the muscle underneath.

"Someone hexed the cash. Probably on some kind of time release. It burned her hand, she swerved, hit the tree, and knocked herself out." Someone who knew Chastity and knew she'd search the pastor's desk for more cash also knew she wouldn't be able to resist the extra cash. The seven deadly sins killer had struck again. This time though, like Janice, Chastity still breathed. But if Janice Heger's second murder attempt was anything to go by, Chastity was still at risk.

Braun's patrol car screeched to a halt near the accident. Zach's deputy brothers scrambled out from a second cruiser and narrowly missed being hit by the healer's ambulance.

"Is she still alive?"

Lila jerked as the bear shifter appeared behind her shoulder. She nodded. "She is, at least for the moment."

"Can you tell me what happened? Winifred's account was a little garbled."

"The pastor bribed Chastity to leave town."

"And she took the money?"

"To the tune of twenty thousand dollars and a wad of hexed bills."

"Can you prove it?"

"There's a cheque shoved down her bra and the hand holding the cash is burned. There will be traces on the money so I wouldn't touch it if I were you."

Braun nodded and collected the cash in an evidence bag. He moved Lila out of the way as the healers went to work.

"If the killer realizes she's still alive, he'll try for a second time. Like Janice."

"I'll make sure there's a guard on the door."

Lila tapped her chin. "What if it doesn't get out?"

"That someone tried to kill Chastity in a car accident?"

"That she survived." Lila put a hand on Zach's arm. "If the killer thinks she's dead, he won't come after her. You can't cover up the accident. There are too many people involved. But you can control the story of her condition."

He caught on. "She died in the car crash and the killer moves on to his next target."

"It's the seven deadly sins. So far, the killer has used pride, lust, gluttony, sloth, and now greed. Wrath and envy are the only ones left. And I have a few ideas who might be the next targets."

"You want to set a trap." Braun rubbed his head. "This feels like a bad idea. You're a Harrow. Bad luck follows you around like a nasty smell."

Lila winked. "Trust me. I have a plan."

"Famous last words."

Hopefully the bear shifter wasn't right. But one way or another, the killer had to be stopped.

EIGHTEEN

"This is your great plan?" Holly hissed as she moved the mini goat cheese tarts from a baking tray to a small platter.

"Trust me. This will work. Now get back to it." Lila crawled under a movable work bench. One of the twins had rigged up drawstring curtains to cover the shelving underneath the trolley. Matthew had even removed the second shelf so Lila could fit under. She cursed as she folded herself into the fetal position. It seemed like a great hiding place for a sleuth on a killer hunt, but not quite so comfortable in practice.

"Are you okay under there, Lila?" Ruby whispered.

"I'm good. Keep an eye out for anything suspicious." The church meeting seemed like the best place to stage a trap. Ezekiel Moss and the Church of the Repentant Creatures were at the center of the whole drama. The church meeting held at the Academy Hall was a prime hunting ground for an obsessed killer.

"Do both of our grandmother's behaviors qualify as suspicious?" Rose carefully drew out a tray full of lobster pot pies and transferred them to a rack to cool slightly.

"That means the apocalypse is nigh." Holly hoisted a platter up. "Do I get paid for this? I could do with some extra spending money."

"Get out there. Braun and Grim are waiting outside for our signal. When we pinpoint the killer, they'll storm the hall. And Elspeth's primed with an immobilizing hex if we need it."

Ruby bit her lip. "I'm not sure why our grandmother insisted on coming tonight. She has no clue about the plan."

"Probably because she heard Elspeth would be here." Holly rolled her eyes. "Those two are predictable." She swung the kitchen door open and marched out.

Rose finished moving the pot pies and dumped the tray in the sink. "I don't think that's it. She rang up one of her old Portland friends last night. 'Was on the phone with her for hours. Delilah seemed closed off when she finished the call. Not her usual upbeat self, then Gran announced she'd be attending the meeting. She definitely wasn't acting like herself. I'm worried she might be involved somehow." Rose bit her lip and blinked her eyes rapidly.

"Do you think she's the killer?" Lila knew Elspeth would defend her family, no matter the consequences. Was Delilah similar or could she kill for other reasons?

"No." Ruby raised her voice a little. "Delilah has a lot of flaws, but unlike the rest of our family, she wouldn't kill without provocation. I'm sure she isn't the killer. But our grandmother's definitely up to something."

Lila slapped the side of the trolley. "Well, get me out there. It's time to spy out a killer."

Rose grabbed the pot pies and arranged them across the top of the bench. "Let's get cracking." She grunted as she tried to move the mobile bench. "No offence, Lila, but maybe it's time for a diet."

Seriously, the twins were as much work as Holly. "Release the brake."

"Oops." Rose giggled and flicked the brake off. The bench surged forward, hitting the kitchen door.

Squeaking, Lila held on. Hard to find good sleuthing help these days.

"Sorry," Rose whispered and carefully moved Lila out into the hall. She positioned the bench next to the buffet table, which had an extra-long tablecloth covering it. Rose lifted the pot pies onto the serving table then stood in front of the bench and clapped her hands. "Dinner is served. The lobster pot pies need a few moments to sit, but please feel free to eat at your own leisure. Various side dishes are now available on the buffet table as well. Please enjoy."

Lila slid out from the end of the movable bench and crawled under the main table. The tablecloth went clear to the ground, which meant no chance of anyone spotting her lurking underneath.

"Doesn't this look delicious. Such a cut above the normal fare in town." Delilah strolled over to the table.

Lila peaked from underneath the tablecloth and spotted the Devlin matriarch's shell pink-colored toes in white sandals. The urge to poke the woman's pretty toes with a sharp implement clawed at Lila. She took a deep breath and focused on the sleuthing problem at hand. Find a killer. The church group squabbled among themselves, debating over who had the right to plan the next activity. Agnes's and Horace's voices rose. Agnes in a masculine, military style jacket pointed at Horace and he whacked her finger away, but certainly, no sign of a killer. Yet.

"Always an opinion, even when it's wrong." Elspeth stomped up to the table in lavender combat boots.

Delilah trilled a high-pitched laugh. "Elspeth, what a fashion delight you are."

"Better than being a psychotic love leech."

"Now, ladies. We all agreed before we sat down to be civil." Pastor Moss smiled benignly and placed a hand on each woman's shoulder. "Besides, you both look lovely tonight. I'd hate for you two to ruin your outfits with a wrestling fight."

"Ezekiel, what a charmer you are." Delilah linked arms with the man and drew him away from Elspeth. "I'm sure dear Elspeth would never allow herself to soil her fashions." Delilah led Ezekiel away to a deserted corner of the room.

"That woman's going down even if I have to hex her hair conditioner."

"Sweet cheeks, you're my pick every time. Not that no-meat-on-her-bones man eater." Colin wandered up and sat at Elspeth's feet. "Feed me, babe? It's better to be primed if the enemy's lurking.

You know how fast I can clear a room if there's danger." Colin scratched his back, then lowered his head to the floor and sniffed. "You know what? I smell sugar." He snuffled up to the tablecloth and shoved his head underneath. "Hey, what do you know. The nose is never wrong."

"Except, I'm not sweet. I'm undercover. Now get out." Lila shoved Colin's head out from her hiding space.

"Man, finally find some sugar, and it turns out to be bitter. What a pill."

Elspeth rubbed her minion's head. "Never mind, darling boy. I'm sure Delilah brought Kali, why don't you stalk her? It'll make you feel better."

"That's why you're the Queen of mayhem, babe." Colin trotted off, little pug tail wagging.

"That poodle will eat him alive."

"Hush, baker girl. Tablecloths don't talk." Elspeth loaded her plate up. "If you're wondering, everything seems normal. Delilah's flirting. Agnes and Horace are glaring at each other. And Ezekiel has the three other old biddies eating out of his hand. Nothing suspicious yet."

Burnt butter. She thought by now the killer would have made their move. And she was stuck under this table. Lila bit her lip as a new plan formed. "Start piling plates of food on the bench, Elspeth. Then wheel it around but park the trolley back out of view as far as you can."

"How's that going to help?"

"Because, as you wheel me around and place plates of food on the table, I'll be able to listen into different conversations."

"Risky idea. I love it. Better scoot back to your trolley and I'll start loading up."

Lila crawled quickly to the other end and back under the movable bench. Just in time, as Elspeth expertly flicked the brake and set the trolley moving.

"Stop." Holly screeched, then blushed as the entire meeting stared at her. "Sorry. I was worried Elspeth might damage the trolley. It should stay in place next to the food table."

"No. I think it's a better idea to move it around so people can access the food while they talk. It's the new plan." Elspeth smiled at the room and then turned to Holly and dropped her eyelid in an exaggerated wink.

"I don't think so. The plan was to have it stationary. And what's wrong with your eye?" Holly stepped forward and placed a hand on the bench.

"I think the plan has been updated." Smiling

sweetly, Elspeth stepped up and crunched a combat boot onto Holly's shoe-clad toes.

Smothering Holly's pained shriek with a pretend air kiss, Elspeth peeled her granddaughter's fingers off the trolley. "Leave it to the experts. Your ability to adapt to changing situations needs practice." With that, Elspeth whipped the bench away from Holly and headed for the table. Smiling, she placed different plates of food at strategic positions on the table. Then parked the bench in the hallway. One end of the trolley still within view, but the other pointing away so no one could see Lila sneak out the back if she needed to.

Before escaping her spy house on wheels, Lila peered out. Everyone happily devoured the food. Even flirty Delilah and the pretty pastor had joined the dinner portion of the meeting. Horace seemed to have disappeared though, probably to the men's room on the other side of the hall. He'd been drinking quite heavily from a hip flask for most of the evening. Taking the opportunity, Lila carefully backed out of her mini spy vehicle and hot footed it down the hallway to the back exit. She wanted to make sure her backup was ready outside. Holly and Elspeth could keep an eye out for any suspicious activity. Easing the exit open, Lila slipped out into the cool night air.

"Aren't you supposed to be stalking the meeting?"

Lila bit a screech back as Matthew appeared next to her. "Can't you put a bell on or something? I nearly had a heart attack."

"A bell isn't covert, and I wouldn't give you a heart attack. Your love of sugar will do that. How's it going in there?" Matthew drew Lila against his chest and wrapped his arms around her.

Heat washed up Lila's throat and she angled her head back. "Holly and Elspeth almost came to blows over me, Colin's stalking Kali, and everyone else would rather eat than attempt a murder. Tonight could be a bust"

"Enough fraternizing." Xandie stomped up to the couple. "I hope my objection is on record for involving the Devlins in our operation."

"That's jealousy talking." Lila poked her tongue out at her cousin. "Now get back in place and tell Braun to get ready. I'm not going to give up tonight yet, but I do need a secret bathroom break before there's a major incident."

Squeezing Matthew's arm, Lila slipped out of his embrace and snuck around the side of the building.

Earlier in the night, she'd Elspeth crack the restroom window wide open and had placed an upturned trash can underneath. She should be able to shimmy through and into the restroom undetected if her hips didn't catch like last time. Lila gathered herself under the open window but ducked as someone strolled into the restroom. She held her breath. Whoever it was whistled as they washed their hands. The door opened a second time and someone else entered.

"I like your meeting place. Unexpected, of course. I would never have thought someone like you would want to meet in a lady's bathroom. But I can touch up my makeup while I make some money, so it's a win-win situation. That delightful boy Ezekiel commented on how lovely I looked tonight. One must keep up appearances. Don't you think so?"

Sounded like Delilah Devlin was conducting a spot of blackmail business. Lila wondered why Delilah was making such a big deal about meeting in the ladies' bathroom. Unless the person Delilah was meeting with wouldn't normally be seen in a lady's restroom... Like a man? Lila focused back on the conversation, listening intently.

"Cat got your tongue? Not speaking to me? I am happy to do the talking. Something familiar about you nagged me when I first got here. I mean, I've known a lot of people in my time." Delilah trilled a piercing laugh. "But it finally came to me where I'd met you. Such a coincidence to run into you here in Point Muse." Delilah waited for a few moments before continuing, "Still the silent sulking type I see. Let me spell it out. Unless you want me to spill your dirty little secret, you'll recompense me handsomely for keeping my mouth shut. Think it over."

From the kissing noises Lila heard from underneath the window, Delilah must've blown air kisses to her blackmail target. The noise of the door opening and closing twice spurred Lila to poke her head up a little bit and take a quick peek. The restroom appeared empty. Lila listened for another few minutes before deciding to move. She hauled herself up and into the restroom. Rushing to the door, she peeped out, making sure the coast was clear before scooting back to her mobile spy station. Settling herself back into place, Lila waited for Elspeth to appear. Her grandmother was all knowing and would have seen her sneak back in. The bench jolted forward as someone pushed it.

"I've got it, Horace. I'll take the trolley back to the kitchen."

"You don't think I can be useful, Elspeth?

There's a lot of things you don't know about me," Horace snarled at the Harrow matriarch.

"I could care less about you, Horace. I'm just here to help."

Someone must've grabbed hold of the handle of the trolley and yanked, because the wheeled workbench shot forward at a fast pace.

"Since when do you help those demented Devlins?"

"I'm helping out the Pastor, not the Devlins. This is his meeting, isn't it?" Elspeth spat.

The bench flew backward and forward. Lila closed her eyes as her stomach rose to greet her throat. She gripped the metal frame, hanging on tightly.

"Would you two please calm down," Agnes scolded both Horace and Elspeth.

"Shut it, Agnes," Horace roared. "I've had enough of keeping quiet."

"Now you speak?" Delilah strolled up.

Lila froze. That sounded like confirmation from Delilah that Horace had been the person she'd black mailed. What had he done? Could he be the killer?

"Stay out of my business, Devlin."

"With all the noise you three are making, it's everyone's business. As it's my granddaughters' catering night, why don't I take the trolley back?" Delilah grabbed the trolley and yanked hard. It teetered for a moment, then hit the ground with a slam.

Lila bit a scream back, as her head bounced off the metal frame.

"That's it, Devlin. I've had enough," Elspeth hollered.

The sound of something wet hitting a solid object followed by Delilah's scream echoed through the room.

"Two can play at this game, Harrow."

Again, the sound of squelching accompanied by a roar filled the room. Soon multiple wet noises surrounded Lila.

"Hang on," Holly whispered.

Lila gripped the metal frame tight as the trolley was righted and quickly wheeled to the kitchen.

Holly whipped up one of the coverings on the side and exposed Lila. "All good. We're in the kitchen."

Crawling out, Lila sat on the floor and rubbed her head with a wince. "Hecate's roller coaster. What happened?"

"Horace and Elspeth had a fight over the trolley.

Delilah joined in, and Elspeth started a food fight as a distraction," Holly recited.

Ruby sighed. "At least we got paid. Earlier. Any sign of the killer yet?"

"No, but I'm sorry. I heard Delilah blackmail someone. Horace, I think."

"I knew Delilah planned something. That phone call was a dead giveaway." Rose blew out her breath.

Holly peered out at the food tornado that had destroyed the interior cleanliness of the hall. "Should we get out there and stop the food fight?"

"No way am I putting a target on my back. Besides, I'm still undercover."

"Kind of a perfect distraction for a killer to grab his next target, don't you think?" Holly turned and stared at Lila, her eyes flickering silver to amber then back again to a solid silver. Her voice deepened. "You should check on Elspeth, Lila. No need for undercover anymore."

The banshee's voice hung in the air, prodding Lila into action. When the banshee spoke, a Harrow listened. Pushing herself up, Lila threw undercover to the wind and bolted out into the hall. The food fight still labored on with a few stubborn food throwers taking aim.

Colin galloped through the sticky mess on the

floor and skidded into Lila's legs. "Sweet cheeks, my dame has disappeared along with that scrawny chicken, Delilah. I've got a bad vibe, babe, and I'm not even hungry."

Scanning the room, Lila realized the pug was right. No sign of Delilah or Elspeth. "When did you last see them?"

"That good-looking man from the church took them outside to calm down. Then a couple of churchies left. And the rest kept playing with their food."

"Right, Colin. Race out the back and let Braun know what's happened. I'm checking out the front." Without waiting to see if the pug followed her orders, Lila turned and bolted out the front, only to stumble across a prone figure. Lila dropped her knees next to the body. She sighed with relief when she realized the person still breathed. Lila rolled the figure over and exposed an unconscious Pastor Ezekiel. Blood trickled down from a lump at his hairline. "Pastor, can you hear me? Do you know where Delilah and Elspeth are?"

The pastor groaned, mumbling a word over and over.

Lila leaned in close and strained to make out his mumbled words.

His eyes flickered and his gaze focused on Lila for a moment. "Church." He croaked out the word and then lowered his head with another groan as Ruby and Rose gathered in close.

Lila looked up at the twins. "The killer has our grandmothers."

Time for another Harrow rescue mission.

NINETEEN

"Shouldn't we wait for the boys? This is what they trained for." Rose gripped Ruby's hand tight.

"Firstly, Braun is trained for it. Secondly, Matthew's a reaper. He's trained in reaping souls, not hostage negotiation."

"And bakers are?"

Lila glared at Holly. "Where's your Harrow backbone, girls?"

Rose held her hand up. "Devlin, remember?"

"Find your nasty streak then. Elspeth and Delilah are in the church. The only way the killer could've taken them down was to knock them out with one of Elspeth's hexes. Otherwise, those witches would've eaten the killer alive."

"I'm primed. Let me at the villain who took my

Queen," Colin growled and pawed the ground like a miniature bull.

Kali, Delilah's poodle, opened her mouth wide, showing sharp white teeth.

Next to her, Nash, Lila's hellhound, let his eyes flicker red and his hackles rose.

"Okay." Lila held her hand up. "I get it. You want to join the rescue party. But we have to be smart about it. The killer's one teaspoon of sugar short. We have to be crafty. We need to follow our plan."

"You need to wait for law enforcement." The reaper loomed over Lila's shoulder; arms folded.

"Wow. Put a black hoodie on you and you look just like the Grim Reaper. Get it?" Lila's smirk wilted. "Fine. You're here. Great. But you aren't stopping us from going in. We were here first and it's our evil grandmothers."

Ruby and Rose stepped up next to Lila, the same mulish expression on their faces.

Matthew glared at the trio, then turned his attention to Holly. "Don't you have something to say? How are you all going to storm the church and rescue Elspeth without anyone getting hurt?"

Holly blanched. "Are you kidding me? There's a truly evil and wicked person in there... And a killer and Delilah too. It's danger central. I'm not going in there."

"Wimp," Lila coughed into a fist.

"Look, Braun and his deputies will be here any second. He'll handle everything."

"About that?" Xandie strolled up, her mother and her two aunts with her. "We've decided this is a Harrow issue. The family's handling the takedown, and you guys get the killer all trussed up. Just like a special homicidal present."

"You called in the big guns?"

Lila winked at her boyfriend. "What's the point of our family having a rep if we don't use it?" She patted a dumb-founded Matthew on the back. "And I'm sorry. Really sorry. We do have a plan, if it's any consolation."

"None whatsoever. Why are you so sorry?" Matthew narrowed his eyes. "What have you got planned?"

"I'm sorry for this." Lila nodded at Holly who produced a hot pink water balloon and threw it at Matthew's legs.

"What the..." Matthew jerked. "Tell me you didn't."

Lila pointed at Holly. "I didn't. She did. You got distracted by her scaredy-cat act. You really should've expected something dodgy from a Harrow, even a whiny one."

"What's happening?" Rose whispered to sister and clasped her hand tight.

Xandie stepped forward, a neutral expression on her face as she addressed the twins. "We knew Elspeth might be a target, same as Delilah. We planned for an abduction, just in case. Lila had a stash of Elspeth's hexes hidden away in her van and Holly just used a paralyzing hex on the reaper's legs."

Miranda Harrow, Xandie's mother, stepped forward. A sleek black rifle with a scope held loosely at her side. "I'm on the perimeter in case of a runner. My sisters and Xandie are on police duties. Lila, Holly, and the dogs are the breach party."

Rose dropped Ruby's hands. "Ruby can stay with Xandie, but I'm sticking with Lila. Delilah is hard to deal with when riled up. You'll need me there."

Lila nodded. "Let's get into position then." She threw some hex balloons at Rose. "Catch."

Rose bobbled the balloons but managed to snag them and clasp them to her chest.

"Lila," Matthew growled.

Her stomach flip-flopped and Lila bit her lip as

she shuffled toward the reaper. "It had to be done. There's no way you would've let me storm the church."

Matthew nodded, a stoic expression on his face. "You're right. But you could've trusted me. You put thought into a plan and have the whole Harrow family involved instead of rushing in and winging it like most of the time. You should have spoken to me."

"I know. And I'm sorry. But it just got out of control. I understand if you're not interested in seeing me anymore after this. But I had to do it."

"You're an idiot, Lila. I'm not going to stop seeing you just because you freeze me and want to run into a treacherous hostage situation. You're actually being responsible for once. Mind you, I could do without the paralyzing hex. I have a fierce itch in my toes that I can't reach and it's frustrating. Just next time, give me a heads up. You might be surprised at my reaction."

Lila leaned against her rigid boyfriend. "Does that mean you're not going to throw me away like a deflated soufflé?"

"It means you and I will go on a holiday away from family and Point Muse. Got it, Harrow?"

She pressed a kiss to Matthew's beaky nose. "It's

a date. Now I have to go and raid a church and rescue my wicked witch grandmother. Back soon."

Xandie nodded to Lila. "We'll guard him, and I'll handle Braun. He'll be here any minute, so scoot."

Nodding, Lila scooted out from the tree line behind the church. The dogs, Holly, and Rose followed as Lila headed for the kitchen door.

Holly grabbed Lila's hand and jerked her to a stop. "There's another door. Mom told me about it. A small side door that opens into the vestibule where the Pastor changes. You head there, Rose and I will come through the kitchen and go around the other side of the church."

Lila nodded. "Okay, Kali, stay with Rose and Holly. I'll take Nash and Colin. Holly, hit the highlights of the plan for Rose. Let's go." Lila followed Holly's directions and the skinny door stood exactly where she'd said. She eased the door open slowly. Did no one lock the doors in Point Muse anymore?

Three little steps led to a small room behind the stage where the pastor preached from. Another door let out into the church proper, alongside the stage.

"Is my girl okay? Can you see her?" Colin rubbed against Lila's legs, his body vibrating with worry.

Nash prowled around the room, lifting his head

every now and then to scent the air. His eyes flickered red. "Prey," the hellhound growled.

Lila knelt next to Nash and rubbed his head. "Remember the plan, boys?"

Colin puffed out his chest. "Colin, the magnificent, is ready to go. I will rescue my Queen and she will feed me."

"I think you had enough to eat at the church meeting."

The pug grimaced. "That lobster's better out than in. Best I use my skills for evil rather than good."

Standing, Lila gave Nash one last head rub. "That's why you're in on the rescue. We can use your upset stomach as our secret weapon. Now, use the shadows. The goal is to free Elspeth and Delilah and bring the killer down. Got it?"

Nash licked his lips. "Prey lose," he growled.

The hellhound had his priorities in order. Putting a finger to her lips, Lila cracked the door open and rolled two hexes out onto the floor next to the stage. On the other side of the room, she knew Holly and Rose would be doing the same. And if everything went according to plan, dark shadows would be covering the inside of the church within five minutes.

Dense black shadows, just like Elspeth's, shot out from the hex bombs and quickly covered the floor of the church. Lila nodded at the dogs, who crept out until the shadows hid them.

Lila followed the canines out and dropped to her hands and knees, crawling under the shadows as much as she could. She paused at the end of the wall where the little hallway on the side of the stage gave way to open space and church pews. She peered around the corner. The killer had shoved pews away and created a big circle in the middle of the room. Elspeth and Delilah sat trussed up on spindly wooden chairs, with the killer standing behind them. "I told you no tricks, Elspeth. I've seen how devious you can be."

"Bah. I'm much more devious than that old wicked witch." Delilah glared at her fellow bound hostage.

"I can't help it. When I get nervous, I produce shadows. It's a natural bodily action." Elspeth wriggled in her chair. "Don't you raise your voice to me, Delilah Devlin. This is all your fault anyway."

"You evil witch. How dare you say that falsehood?" Delilah wrenched her bonds, trying to attack Elspeth.

The killer paced around the squabbling duo. "Do

you really think I'm so stupid? I know you two hate each other, but I can also see you testing your bonds at the same time." The killer waggled her fingers at the pair. "I'm sorry you got involved, Elspeth. But you really should have stayed away from Ezekiel. Once he paid attention to you, well... You had to go. Delilah started it all, didn't you? Swanning into my town, with not a care in the world. Quietly destroying everything I had built... Again."

"See, it's all Delilah's fault." Elspeth glared at her nemesis.

"I've decided you'll be wrath and envy. Although really, I'm taking you two down with the same hex. And you should be happy, Elspeth. It's one of your specialties." The killer read the label of the spray bottle she held up. "Vitriol Hex."

Lila winced. That was one of Elspeth's nastier hexes. Spray it on your victim and they were consumed by fury and malice. It was like a sulfuric acid for the soul and literally burnt out a person's insides unless they were administered the antidote within half an hour of infection. She needed to get out there and stop the killer before it went that far. Taking a breath, and hoping the others were in place, Lila stood and walked toward the killer. "What was your plan next, Agnes? Or should I call you by your real name, Sherry?"

Agnes spun around and bared her teeth. "I knew a Harrow would turn up. But I honestly thought it would be the Librarian. She seems smarter than the rest of you."

"Not this time." Lila strolled forward. The shadows had reached midthigh. Perfect for creeping dog assassins.

Raising the spray bottle, Agnes threatened her hostages. "No closer, dear. I'd hate for this to go off and kill your grandmother. The other one I have no problems with." She pointed the spray bottle at Delilah.

"I have an issue with that. She's wicked but she is my grandmother." Rose stood on the other side of the church, Holly nowhere to be seen.

"Another Devlin. You're like cockroaches, no matter how one stamps you out you always pop up."

"Sherry, this is revenge for stealing and killing your husband, I take it," Delilah said.

"My name isn't Sherry. I'm not her anymore," Agnes screamed.

"And I never killed Herb. He was lovely to me. I broke it off with him only because of you. I thought we'd all be safer from your psychotic episodes if we weren't together."

"No. No. This is all your fault." Agnes wavered on her feet, her mental psychosis taking hold. "I loved my Herb, until you ruined him. He left me for you, told me I wasn't half the woman you were," Agnes cackled, a pale imitation of Elspeth. "I decided if I couldn't have Herb, no one would, especially not Delilah Devlin. I went to a hex expert, and he gave me a tincture of the Ephedra. Said it would work a treat. I borrowed a glamour off him and made sure I looked like Delilah. I organized a date and Herb actually thought you wanted to get back together." Agnes shook her head.

"Then you poisoned him." Delilah sagged in her bonds.

"Oh, not just him. All those idiots who panted after dear Ezekiel had to go too."

"The seven deadly sins."

Agnes nodded her approval at Lila. "I thought it appropriate. Each one of those women deserved to die. Ezekiel is mine, no one else's."

Rose strolled closer. "We opened our shop and put a spanner in the works. The Devlin name scared you. You thought you'd be discovered."

"And then I hit town. Must've put the fear of

God in your defective brain, Sherry." Delilah smirked. "Ask Elspeth, I have a talent for annoying people."

Elspeth nodded. "She does, trust me."

Agnes hissed like a cat. "I lost half of my body weight, stopped dyeing and straightening my hair, and wore contacts. I had a whole new life. Then Delilah Devlin strolls into my town. I knew she'd tell her granddaughters all about me. I came up with a plan to frame them for poisoning Lila's customers." Agnes frowned, confused. "I honestly thought the first thing the Police Chief would do is arrest the Devlins." She turned to Lila, apologetic. "I really do like you. But I underestimated the hold those Devlins have over men."

Lila shrugged and moved closer. "I'm not worried. Elspeth will come up with a hex to counteract it. We can't have those Devlin girls stealing our men, can we?"

"No. You're right. I always thought you were a decent soul, Lila Harrow."

Out of the corner of her eye, Lila spotted a little pug tail weaving toward the hostages, while a black hound stalked Agnes.

"Elaine and Laura-Jean? Lust and pride, I suppose."

"Of course. That loudmouth whiner and her beautiful red hair and that oversexed Elaine. She carried on with that horrible Horace Painter and made goo-goo eyes at the Pastor." Agnes spat on the ground. "She thought she owned Ezekiel, the hair flipping, the winks, the little touches. I couldn't stand it. When I saw the Devlins, I thought I could kill two annoying birds with one cake."

"But you missed with Laura-Jean and had to go back again with a gluttony hex. That was sloppy, and then it happened again with poor Janice and Chastity. Shame it didn't work with Chastity." Lila tilted her head slightly at Rose, who readied herself.

Colin reached Elspeth's chair and gnawed at her bonds.

"Chastity's alive?" Agnes screamed and flung her arms wide, accidentally coating Elspeth and Delilah with a small amount of the Vitriol Hex.

Lila was out of time, she had to push Agnes over the edge. "Awake and perky, happily flirting with the doctors at the hospital. We made sure no one realized she'd survived the accident. We beat you, Sherry."

"I am. Not. Sherry." Agnes dropped the spray bottle to the ground and raised her clenched fists into the air. Veins on the side of her forehead throbbed.

A figure, smothered in a black hooded coat, with

burning silver eyes, blazed a path through the shadows, her blazing white canine at her side. "You can't shed the soul you were born with, Sherry. But you can learn and strive for worthiness." The black coat parted, and a silver sword flashed in the shadows of the church.

Squealing, Agnes backpedaled, arms flailing. "Azrael, Angel of Death. Spare me," she shrieked and covered her ears. Stepping back, Agnes tripped over Nash who'd crept up behind the woman. The killer hit the ground, screaming as the Angel of Death with her shining silver sword, a red-eyed hellhound, and a white glowing poodle stood over her.

"Hit the lights, Rose, and let the cavalry know we've got the killer contained."

Colin spat out a mouthful of Elspeth's bonds as he released her. "Can someone untie the chicken, my teeth hurt."

"If anyone mentions my good deed of untying Delilah, I'll curse you with dirty laundry for eternity." Elspeth shoved herself out of her chair and crouched behind Delilah muttering. "Curtain ties. That crazy nut-bag tied us up with curtain ties from the church. We'll never live this down."

Delilah rubbed her wrists as the front door of the

church flung open and the backup raced inside, led by their grandchildren.

"We will never speak of this, Harrow." Delilah glared at Elspeth. "Kidnapped with a Harrow by a religious obsessed fanatic, my reputation will suffer."

"Goes ditto for me, love leech."

"We need to get an antidote for that hex she sprayed them with. Otherwise, they'll get meaner until their anger eats their insides."

"About that." Elspeth coughed. "I labelled that spray bottle wrong. It's just vinegar for cleaning."

"We risked our lives for vinegar and you two are just this plain mean normally?" Lila glared at her grandmother.

"You get good karma points for saving us and you even roped in an Angel of Death." Elspeth clapped her hands and the shadows dissipated at the same time as the church lights blazed on.

"Not quite." Lila smirked as the Angel of Death pushed back her hood to expose a giggling Holly wielding a lightsaber with Kali, the poodle, by her side.

"I never thought this would work. The chick must've been pretty far gone."

Braun stomped over to the group with an unfrozen Grim. "Once again, a simple rescue is turned into a drama by the Harrow family. Why can't we just have a simple hostage negotiation for once?"

Xandie slipped in next to her boyfriend and laid her head on his shoulder. "Just wait until the wedding. I'll let you negotiate the hostage situation then."

Elspeth's head snapped to the side. "Did I hear wedding?"

Waggling her hand, Xandie grinned and showed off her ring. "That's why he spent so much time with the Devlins. They have a jeweler friend who helped him pick a ring." She eyed the Devlins hugging each other. "I guess they aren't so bad."

Matthew marched straight to Lila and lifted her off her feet in a tight embrace.

"Please don't tell me you're about to propose too?"

He chuckled, a deep barrel laugh. "Not yet."

Lila stared shocked at her boyfriend. Did he just imply...

Holly started hooting and slapping her leg. "That's perfect. Now Elspeth will start nagging you guys about kids. See what you've let yourselves in for?"

The cousins stared at Holly, open mouthed.

Xandie broke the silence. "You do realize you're the only one single. I'm engaged and Lila's as good as. You're Elspeth's matchmaking dead meat. I'd start running now."

The light saber dropped with a clang to the ground, surprising Agnes, who stopped mumbling and tried to crawl away.

"Geronimo." Colin jumped on the woman's back, spreading her flat on the ground. "I'm ready to go. Evacuation protocols," Colin roared, and the church emptied. Even the brave hellhound and the vicious poodle bolted like fleeing rats.

Lila elbowed Grim and he dropped her to the ground and dashed past. There was no solidarity when it came to Colin's radioactive flatulence. She snagged Holly's hood on the way out and dragged her shell-shocked cousin down the front steps. Just in time as Colin exploded.

A lobster-scented, green radioactive aroma wafted through the church, along with the agonizing wail of an olfactory tormented Agnes.

The killer had been apprehended. Brought to justice. And now suffered for her crimes...

A stench worse than death.

TWENTY

"She put my profile up on E-Supe. My inbox is full of weird, kinky emails, telling me how much they want to play with my lightsaber." Holly raised bleary, bloodshot eyes. "How did she get a picture anyway? Wasn't she tied up at the time?"

Xandie cleared her throat. "That was my fault. I had Zach snap a photo for posterity." She defended her actions. "I'd just gotten engaged. Hormones were popping. I thought it was sweet you dressed up for a hostage rescue."

"It. Was. The. Plan," Holly ground out.

"We did warn you," Lila pointed out fairly. "But you were too busy laughing at us to listen. You have an Elspeth target on your back. There's no dodging the matchmaking now. Resign yourself to your fate."

"Elspeth Harrow can kiss my britches." Holly sat up, eyes fired with determination. "I won't be led around by my hormones, unlike you two. Only death interests me."

Xandie and Lila scooted their chairs back and Lila motioned for another plate of whoopie pies from Ruby. "You are so going down, Holly Harrow. Never sass Elspeth or challenge her unless you have heavy artillery. You'll always lose." Lila didn't need a banshee to predict an all-out chaos war between Harrows.

May the best Harrow win...

The End.

* * *

Want More?

You can sign up for my mailing list. It's for new releases and no spam. Be the first to grab specials, new releases and freebies.

Sign up now.
https://www.kellyethan.com/newsletter

Did you like this book?

Please leave a review for it on Amazon!
Sin, Sugar and Shadows

I want to thank everyone who spent the time to read my novel.

My world is small town magic, mystery and mayhem, with plenty of snarky laughs along the way.

With an overactive imagination and a love of all things that go bump in the night, it was natural to write cozy paranormal mysteries, but I also love paranormal romance. No matter the genre, I love sarcastic heroines who like to save the day and solve the puzzle.

With a busy and chaotic household, writing is my outlet for madness. I live in Australia and when not writing, I can be found plotting my next fictional murder or chasing after the family's ferocious hellhound.

Visit me today at my website or say hello on social media.

Website:
https://www.kellyethan.com

#8 The Nefarious Nemesis and the Wedding Jinx

Point Muse Cozy Paranormal Mystery Boxed Set: Books 1-3

Point Muse Cozy Paranormal Mystery Boxed Set: Books 4-6

Point Muse Cozy paranormal Mystery Boxed Set: Books 1-8

LILA HARROW: Point Muse Cozy Paranormal Mystery

Cookies, Curses and Christmas Corpses.

#1 Cupcakes, Corpses and Chaos

#2 Pies, Potions and Peril

#3 Sin, Sugar and Shadows

LILA HARROW Point Muse Boxed Set: Books 1-3

HOLLY HARROW: Point Muse Cozy Paranormal Mystery

Banshee, Vikings and Voodoo

#1 Banshee, Death and Disarray

#2 Banshee, Moonshine and Madness

#3 Banshee, Sea Monster and Sabotage

HOLLY HARROW Point Muse Boxed Set: Books 1-3

The Ghost Vein Mine Cozy Paranormal Mysteries

#1 Ghosts and Gold Dust

#2 Curses and Cold Cases

Non Fiction

Heart and Craft.

www.ingramcontent.com/pod-product-compliance
Lightning Source LLC
Chambersburg PA
CBHW051303210726
48287CB00002B/650